HORROR SCOPE

HORROR SCOPE

ART McCONNELL

COVER ILLUSTRATION BY
CASSIDY BECK & TOM SILVINO

BOOK DOMAIN LLC
Publish to Perfection

FOR ALL THE INNOCENTS

THE HORROR SCOPE

The afternoon sunlight filters into the small bedroom where Astrological charts cover most of the wall space. The telephone rings twice activating a recorded message: "You have reached the Zodiac Service, please leave your name, phone number and your Sign and I'll be getting back to you shortly. Thanks for the call, it is important to us." The caller begins but is interrupted as a hand reaches out, lifting the phone from the cradle…

Parker Wilsone has always been a well-educated prodigy. At eighteen he is preparing for Graduate School. He is a valid Chess Master who has competed and won internationally. The boy is also a whiz at Astrology, capable of guessing the birth-dates of people that he has just met, sometimes having not even spoken to them. Let's face it, Parker Wilsone is a brain.

It's his girlfriend Stephanie on the phone. She wants him to come over to her house and help her with some Calculus homework. She also wants to model her new black bikini for him.

An hour later he's at the girl's house, working on the books. They take a break and she removes his eyeglasses and begins rubbing his forehead and temple area. Parker pulls her into him and kisses her sweet face with his mouth partially open. After a while Stephanie jumps up and begins to unbutton her blouse as she asks her boyfriend to check out her new skimpy swimsuit. She then drops her cut-off shorts to the floor as the "Math Genius" watches this shapely seventeen year old strip down to a tiny black bikini. He tells her that the wolves on the beach are going to be drooling all over her as she stands up. Placing his hands on her tight little waist, Stephanie slowly undoes his shirt as they fall down onto the bed together and begin making out. She licks his lips as her straps slide down her studio-tanned arms. The attractive girl's long hair moves from side to side as she kisses her boyfriend with a gentle force.

The next evening Parker rides the train into the city on his way to an Astrology seminar. He carries a leather case with a Zodiac emblem emblazoned on the side. The train stops and a gang of young punks enter the subway car smoking cigarettes and talking loudly. One has a quart bottle of beer; another has a flask of whiskey. One of them walks over to where Parker is sitting and begins to hassle him. The punk grabs the case and Parker struggles against him, taking it back. Other gang members begin to move in as the whiz kid breaks loose and runs through the moving cars of the train as it enters the underground tunnels and the frantic world of darkness shattered by the chaotic flashing lights.

The doors open at a stop in the city and the emotionally distraught Parker runs from the train, then down the long series of metal staircases. He slips on the way down and his briefcase falls a few steps. He reaches out for it but it keeps bouncing down the steps. Parker runs nervously down the stairs to retrieve the case. Ten minutes later the disoriented youth is standing in the cool night, sur-rounded by colorful neon lights. He walks quickly down a darkened side street clutching the leather briefcase under his arm. Wilsone looks around in a paranoid manner as the sound of a siren in the night brings his shoulders up. His intense eyes pan the alleyway.

Three blocks away an elderly black man is being robbed by two men who throw him up against a wall and punch him merci-lessly as he curses them with a fading spirit.

Meanwhile, Parker walks briskly past a parked Police car, turn-ing his collar up as the night wind hits him. He turns a corner, walks fifty feet or so, and then rounds another to find an elderly black man slumped down against the side of a building. Parker turns at angle near an adjacent alleyway but the man suddenly rolls over showing a large knife pro-truding from his stomach.

Parker stops in his tracks, torn between helping the severely injured senior citizen or taking flight.

In a weak voice the man in agony says,"Help me son, they stabbed me and left me here to bleed and die… please do something boy, this old man can't take the pain." Parker looks around undecid-edly as he walks over to the man on the ground with reluctance. A long silence passes before he finally reaches down and pulls the eight inch steak knife out of the belly of the mortally wounded man, who says, "I can't take the pain any-more…I can't take the pain," in his dying breath.

A car drives down the back alley street turning on it's brights as the vehicle gets closer to Parker and the dead man. The youth freezes as the Police car pulls up and two cops emerge with pistols drawn and ready. He freaks out and runs down a short narrow alley to a dead end throwing his hands up against the cinder block wall.

"This is not happening," he repeats under his breath as the Police bring his hands down behind him, cuffing him securely.

The squad car slowly drives away with Parker Wilsone in the back seat as the body of the old black man is loaded into the Emergency Service Medical van. Flashing lights illuminate the faces in the crowd gathering at the crime scene which is cordoned off with yellow tape containing the word CRIME SCENE continuously printed on it. Parker looks out at the bright lights of the city as the Police car returns to its precinct. He begins to realize that his entire life has changed in this one instance. Although highly intelligent, the boy is alone and scared, not to mention that he's in a mild state of shock.

They arrive at the station house where he's questioned in the interrogation room by a Detective Lawrence,who's out to nail him for this crime against an elderly man. "Come on kid, now quit telling us a fairytale will ya'? You're placed at the scene of the crime with the murder weapon in your hand by two police officers. Coincidence, right?"

"I didn't do it," an upset Parker Wilsone reports. "The old man must have been stabbed just before I got there. He begged me to help him. He kept saying that the pain was too much, so I pulled out the knife. Now his pain has become mine. I'm sorry I ever turned that corner… and this is not a fairytale, it's a freaking nightmare," yells Parker.

"Take it easy, Wilsone. We're gonna' book you, you'll be locked up overnight and we'll see if you change your tune by morning."

Det. Lawrence tells the officer who comes to take Parker to contact the kid's family.

Parker is then removed from the Interrogation Room by officers who walk him down the long hallway where he is placed in a small cell alone. As the steel door closes loudly, re-echoing through the corridors, the young prodigy covers his face with his hands and begins to sob in the cold little room comprised of cinder block and steel while in another part of the facility, a Policeman opens Wilsone's leather case and removes astrological charts and computerized data along with a notebook of his clients.

Parker is unable to make the high bail set for him so he remains in jail where he faces harassment from the hard-core street people who are behind bars with him. He also begins taking anti-depressants for his newly acquired condition brought on by confinement. A week later in the Day Room, two of the local bad boys get into Parker's shit. A muscled-up dude named Jake antagonizes the weak youth with, "You, white boy, you must have felt good knifin' that poor old bastard, huh?" as he looks around laughing to the others.

"I never did the crime, I'm a victim of circumstance, damn it!" Parker replies. Jake's friend Spider is quick to come back with, "Who you bullshitin' Holmes; we all in here 'cause we went and broke the precious laws of society. Now why don't you just cop to it Parker man?" Then Jake says, "You know Wilsone, I was thinking that the old man could have been my father. What do you say about that, Mr. Zodiac, huh?"

Looking him in the eye Parker says, "Not much." Jake gets pissed and yells, "Why you arrogant son of a bitch. Don't you try to act so white with me boy. I'll put you down bad, you dig?" Then Jake and Spider jump up and start beating on Parker. It seems like a long time before the guards show up to save Parker's ass and stop the fight. The men are separated and Parker Wilsone is put in solitary confinement, where he contemplates suicide. He is currently taking large doses of Paxil and walking in circles on his daily one-hour exercise break in the small adjacent yard with the high cinder block walls. He also gets an hour in the T.V. room alone. Late one afternoon, while watching the tube, a mysterious hooded image of a phantom-like specter appears periodically then subtly fades away. Parker, now spaced out on script drugs goes back to watching the test pattern on the tube. The high pitched noise seems to energize him. Then he sees the image taking shape again and reaches out to touch the glass. The strange eyes glare at him, and then quickly vanish, but a connection has definitely been made in these fleeting moments.

Two days later a group of inmates are gathered around a hot Chess game. Parker walks into the room with his hand bandaged and a purple black eye. He looks over the shoulders of the prisoners to see that Jake and Spider are at war on the board. Jake is losing bad and is about to resign.

"Give it up Homey, you're stuck in the spider's web," says Spider with an elated smile.

"Yeah, I think I'm gonna' have to pack it in here; you got this one, bro'."

"Wait, don't resign yet." The group opens to show Parker Wilsone standing there.

"Eh, what do you know asshole?" questions Spider.

"I know I can beat you in three moves, Spiderman," Parker replies.

Jake promptly tells him, "Shit. Sit down Parker and whip his ass good." Parker enters the game and wins in two moves, and in the days to follow he ends up playing ten opponents simultaneously. Sometimes he plays three boards at a time blindfolded, just for a change of pace. His Chess game has earned the prodigy respect on the tier. They now refer to him as Parkerman, the badass "Chess king of the Zodiac." Spider has even apologized for giving him that beating and has become his loyal Chess student. He tells him, "Damn, Parker man, you're a bad dude on them squares. Do you think I'll ever get to be as good as you are?" Brushing the question aside Parker says, "It's so easy to beat you guys that it makes me feel like a criminal."

It's visitor's day at the jailhouse and Stephanie walks through the metal detector and is then escorted to a seat where she waits for Parker. Fifteen minutes pass and he enters the visiting room. As he moves through the occupied tables, getting closer to Stephanie, the youth notices the tears welling up in her eyes.

She stands as he approaches and they hug for a long time before sitting down across from one another. The girl has worn a short skirt to boost his morale.

"Were you in a fight honey? Your eye doesn't look too good. What's going on in here?"

"This place is retarded. I've got to make bail and get out before trial. I got into it with one of the brothers, but I came back and kicked their butts in the game of Chess, so now they respect me."

"We're working on the bail but it's so high because of the Mayor's crackdown on street crime. It's tough to put it together but we'll do it Parker, I swear. What's the food like in here?"

"It sucks. What did the lawyer say?"

"He's working hard on it," Steph says. "You know the time factors involved."

"I've got to get out of this facility; it's crazy in here, my whole life is passing me by. I constantly think about suicide. This trip is wrecking my mind." Parker leans forward and lowering his voice says, "I'm afraid that something really weird is going to happen." He looks around again from left to right then tells her, "There's an outline of a face in the T.V. tube... I think it's the Devil. He wants me to sell my soul for freedom. You got to help me, I'm hallucinating at night."

"I can't promise anything at this point," she says. "Sounds like your brain is working overtime. Just keep your mind active, it's your greatest asset. You're a genius Parker; don't let them get to you. Use Chess, use the powers of Astrology; do what ever you have to do to get through this nightmare. I had lunch with your parents yesterday. They said they'd be coming to see you the beginning of next week. That'll bring your spirits up."

An announcement that this visit will come to an end in five minutes is heard over the public address system. Parker tells Steph to take care of his computer and reference books. He leans toward her saying, "I love you Steph and always will... no matter what happens in the future." Then an annoying sounding buzzer goes off as they stand and exchange a restrained embrace. Stephanie tells him in parting, "Remember, I'll be there when it's over. I love you too. Take care Parker, take care." She turns heads as she leaves the room.

A few months pass before the young Astrologer finds himself in the packed courtroom waiting for the verdict to go down. Judge

Harold Morton reviews some important paper-work before asking the jury, "Have you reached a verdict?" The men and women of the jury look to the Foreman, a man named Crenna, who tells His Honor, "Yes, we have found the defendant, Parker James Wilsone, guilty as charged." Hearing this, Mrs. Wilsone's head falls onto her husband's shoulder as Stephanie covers her eyes with her hands as she begins to cry. Parker sits stone-faced, void of emotion as the consequential verdict is read. Stephanie looks up to meet his eyes across the court room… the rush of the feelings of separation are agonizing as his girlfriend and parents watch the young man taken away.

A month and a half crawls by as Parker Wilsone prepares for his sentence. During the time he stares into the television screen in the day room when no one else is present. He converses telepathically with the spectral image that his hallucinations project on the screen. His intellectual type of mind begins to contrive a deal with the satanic reaper of souls. Parker cuts a deal with the Devil.

The day inevitably comes when the Chess prodigy sits in the courtroom wearing the prison issue jump suit as he awaits the judge's sentence. He watches with a stern face as the court officer tells all present to rise as Judge Morton enters the room from his chambers. He presides on the bench, squaring off a few sheets of paper. Looking up at the defendant His Honor says, "I realize that you still insist upon your innocence, continuing to claim that you were a victim of circumstance, an unfortunate person who was at the wrong place at the wrong time. This jury, however, has found you guilty of the crime as charged, and it is my duty to sentence you, Parker James Wilsone to death by electrocution for the murder of Simon Watson. Do you have anything to say?" Parker looks back over his shoulder at his girlfriend Stephanie, then turns back to the judge. As he stares into the judge's eyes, Parker Wilsone once again proclaims his innocence saying in a loud unwavering voice, "I did not put the knife in that man… I only removed it to ease his pain." Parker's mom puts her head against his father's shoulder as the burly judge says; "The administration of justice has been done. May God save your soul, Parker Wilsone." The convicted nineteen year-old felon smiles for the first time as the hard wooden gavel comes down, saying, "May GOD save yours", under his breath.

On the other side of town a private investigator named John Matlind reads about the Parker Wilsone case in the morning newspaper, his feet up on the desk in his modest office. He's a mixture of Sam Spade, Mike Hammer and Harper all rolled into one. He operates from an archaic building where the noon sun streams through the Venetian blinds creating patterns on the adjacent walls like something out of an old film 'noir' from the 1940s. Matlind folds the paper in half, shifting in his seat. "Something doesn't sound right here. The guy has sworn innocence since his arrest, passed the polygraph with flying colors; he's got a clean record, a past honor student who graduated High School at fourteen and college at seventeen… and now they're going to burn him. Go figure that one out! The kid is a goddamned brain; it doesn't make sense." Matlind's secretary, Julie looks over at him while still typing at high speed. "You think he's innocent John? I mean, they caught him red-handed. It was the closest that a knife ever came to being a smoking gun."

"I suppose no one really knows but Wilsone himself, with no eye-witnesses present. Everything is just too cut and dry. The timing too with the Mayor and Governor's crackdown on crime, plus the re-instating of the electric chair," says Matlind. "Make some calls Julie, and get me into that execution, I want to see that kid face to face."

"Maybe Parker is innocent and telling the truth," Julie sympathizes.

"That's the feeling I'm getting. No way he knifed that old man, no way."

The small day room is quiet now except for the occasional sound of static made by the old television set whose screen shows the familiar test pattern. Parker sits across from the 'tube' in a small, one-piece plastic chair with rounded corners. His eyelids droop down halfway; his teeth are clenched. Clothed in slippers and a jump suit, his eyes begin to focus on the screen as the image of a subliminal flash appears for split-second intervals. He leans forward squinting his eyes as the liquid-like silver skull is fleetingly illuminated in the dim light. He thinks that he hears a voice, but can't make out what it's saying. It sounds like, "die, die, you don't have to… die." Parker begins to sweat as tears roll down his young face. He speaks softly saying, "I don't want death… I want out and I will surrender anything, including my soul in order to escape the hand of the executioner." At this, the screen flashes a sudden brightness that temporarily blinds Parker and causes him to faint, falling from the chair to the floor. His timely agreement with Lucifer has once and for all been sealed—it's a done deal.

Waking up in the prison hospital, Parker looks at the IV tubes in his arm and realizes they are making a conscious effort to keep him alive until his hour of execution comes.

Perhaps he'll be granted a stay at the eleventh hour. Maybe he will fall victim to the hand of fate as the power switch is brought down. Something in his subconscious mind is bothering him, but he can't place it. Strange people in white uniforms have been giving Parker injections of various drugs during the night and sometimes in the day also. Wilsone doesn't know what societetic venoms are running like a rapid river through the canals of his veins and arteries.He has become increasingly complacent; a slow victim of a series of psychological lobotomies. His once brilliant mind is still aware, though, as he plays a solitaire game of Chess back in his diminutive cell. The cinder block walls are sparsely adorned with a simple calendar, a photograph of Stephanie, Parker's parents and a picture of Jesus with his Sacred Heart and wearing a crown of thorns on his bleeding head drawn on a white handkerchief by a Spanish inmate (one of Parker's better Chess students). Down the narrow corridor, a brother in for capital murder raps a jailhouse poem:

> *"It's the wait. That's what begins*
> *to kill you right away.*
> *The wait is a slow burn."*

"Hear that," another inmate echoes. Parker listens as Spider (his name is actually Lee Roy Spyder) spins his rap web. He speaks very simply and somberly:

> *"Burning slow and sweating deep*
> *A man is woken in his sleep.*
> *Wanting to scream out but suppressing it still,*
> *no one waits when it's time to kill!!*
> *Squinting in pain, hot blaring light*
> *Realizing this is the end of night*
> *The King, the Bishop and Castle are here*
> *Inspecting all eyes he thinks of fear.*
> *Walking quiet they leave the cell*
> *Boarding party for the Gates of Hell.*
> *Clanging of metal, droplet of sweat.*

'The Lord is my Shepherd,'
now you must pay your debt."

Trays of dinner are soon served in each individual cell. Parker stares up at the concrete ceiling as he imagines the positions of constellations in the night sky. He misses his practice of Astrology, even though he's done a few charts for some of the guards. He misses sweet Stephanie… in that hot black bikini. He closes his eyes but sleep never comes; only a vision of his girlfriend as he remembers her best.

Some days drag on, as others speed by. Parker actually believes that he's struck up a deal with some imaginary specter on an old TV tube and that he shall not be executed in exchange for selling out his soul and doing the work of the Devil. In fact, he still holds on to that belief as the prison officers come for him on that last evening. Spider says it best;

"It's about the execution—

"The shuffle of slippers in the corridor green.
One sound remains, one sight to be seen.
A thumping of heartbeat, a strong wooden throne…
no man knows better what is meant by alone.
Elevated steps, three in all;
you must not scream out… try hard not to fall.
Witnesses eight, who like, dinner guests
will stuff themselves with the visions of death.
Then comes the final seating – everyone's ready.
The hand of the warden so rigid and steady.
Ten twenty five, ten twenty-six;
Warden checks the clock out
while Parker counts the ticks."

He walks the walk down that last mile path. What a waste of a brilliant mind. The Chess prodigy sits strapped in tight to 'Ol' sparky.' He cannot hold back his tears as he scans the shadowy faces of the witnesses. Matlind the P.I. shifts forward into the subtle light and his eyes meet with Parker's. He doesn't want to see this kid take the fall for someone who got away that night. The words of the jail-house poet trip down the hallway of the Death Row.

> ***"Ten twenty-seven and the big switch is thrown***
> ***Yo! The critical voltage won't leave you a home.***
> ***Swallowed up in the darkness***
> ***blackness becomes your new-found roam."***

The Warden asks the prisoner for any final words. To which the condemned man responds, "You want to hear last words? My only hope is that those people who wrongfully convicted and put me here will someday pay for their mistake… with their own lives." He looks over at the Warden and says, "I'm ready. Do what you have to do."

The juice is turned on at exactly 10:30 p.m., e.s.t. and the lights blink off and on twice, then everything goes pitch black in the room. Parker laughs out loud in a hideous crazed voice as those present fumble in the darkness for lighters, even the backup generator has failed to do it's job. All of the three entrance ways have somehow been locked. Panic begins to set in on the disoriented audience. Someone produces a flashlight, scanning the room and the gallery of confused and frightened faces. But as they shine the beam on the chair of death, the most important face is missing. A side-door is unlocked and word comes in that the East Coast has suffered a major power outage that also affects Canada and the Great Lakes region. Parker's crazed laugh echoes through the ventilator system of the prison. Meanwhile the Death Row inmates tap out various codes as they communicate in the darkest of tiers.

Some lights are beginning to blink periodically throughout the jail as someone bumps into Matlind in the dark. He turns and ignites his disposable lighter. Parker Wilsone stands there looking into the Private Detective's eyes with a death stare. The lighter goes out as a flashlight is dropped on the floor. Matlind quickly re-strikes the flame, but the man who escaped is gone. The former cop yells out, "Lock the doors," but they all have just been opened. The lights come back, powered by the auxiliary generator that had mysteriously failed before. The overhead fixture lamps show the empty electric chair where Parker Wilsone once sat waiting for a jolt into the next world. Across the room, the prison Warden picks up the broken flashlight that was knocked from his hand as the news breaks of a major electrical blackout in the city tonight.

Parker Wilsone reaches the outer boundary of the prison yard and begins to climb the perimeter fence to freedom. Passing a 'DANGER/HIGH VOLTAGE" sign half-way upthe tall chain-link wall, he sees flashlights beaming at the side doors used by the maintenance staff. He drops down to the ground on the other side, slightly injuring one of his ankles. The lights pass above him as he flattens out in the high weeds; waiting for a chance to cross the narrow road and disappear into the high wooded area beyond. A shapeless black specter watches from the forest as Parker limps along, making his getaway, cursing the judge and jury and swearing violent revenge while he navigates through the moonlit woodlands.

Just after dawn an old pickup truck driven by a local farmer waits for an isolated traffic light to change colors. The farmer turns his head to the left to look at the crossroads. When he turns back he finds a stranger in the cab holding the shotgun from the window rack on him.

"Now take it easy boy, that gun's got a hair trigger."

"Don't make me nervous old man, or you're going to be eating buckshot for breakfast," threatens Parker.

The frightened driver assures his captor, "No problem there young fella. Where you headed?"

"Towards the suburbs, and don't speed or attract attention if you don't want this to be your last ride. This thing got gas?"

"Just filled her up this morning. Did you lose your electric power last night young fella'?" asks the farmer.

"I sure as hell did," rants Parker, laughing wildly as he commands the poor man to "Keep driving the exact speed limit if you know what's good for you." Later that afternoon Parker drives away in the old pickup truck wearing the farmer's bib overalls. He cuts a hard turn, raising a good amount of dust into the air, as he waves to the old man in the orange jump suit and beat up straw hat.

Stephanie stretches out diagonally across her large waterbed wearing only the thin sheet that partially covers her. She rests in a twilight state of sleep occasionally turning from side to side as the cool breeze enters the half-raised window in her room. The young girl stirs as a pebble hits the hardwood floor. The next small stone follows, tapping the window then falling back down to the lawn by Parker's feet. Another toss reaches the higher section of the window; this time the sound of the pebble causes her to open the window, stepping on one of the pebbles that Parker threw, as she does.

Hopping away she sees another hit the window; knowing now that it's him.

"Parker!" she exclaims, sticking her head out of the window." The Police are bound to show up here, you're all over the news broadcasts."

"Get dressed fast and bring the car keys and a bag of food and drinks," demands Parker, trying to keep his voice down in the back yard. When the girl doesn't move right away Parker raises his voice, "Well, are you with me or not in this Stephanie?" Looking down at him she says, "Give me ten minutes to get it together; stay out of sight." He steps behind a large hedge as she closes the upstairs window. Parker crouches low and begins to wait for her to come down. Paranoid thoughts fill his mind. He fears that she might make the call that will turn him in to the Police, perhaps with the notion that it will protect him from himself. Just as he begins to doubt her, she turns the corner carrying two knapsacks and a small bag filled with food and bottled water. Stephanie drops them to the ground as she and Parker embrace, kissing passionately. Steph breaks away saying, "We've got to go now Parker, there's a manhunt on for you."

"Right. Steph, let's get out of here. You drive," he says as the two walk down the driveway to the car. "Where's your parents?" he asks nervously.

"Don't worry, they're out of town."

"Good," he replies, "cause that's where we're going too." The pair drive to the end of Stephanie's block, then turn left into the early morning sun. They listen to music on the radio as the Chevy Blazer cruises west on the expressway. Fifteen minutes later the news report airs. Parker leans forward, turning up the volume as the female newscaster mentions a few local stories that lead up to the major one of the day.

"The Police are working on the bizarre escape of the convicted murderer Parker James Wilsone who disappeared from the electric chair he was about to be executed in during the black-out which occurred just two days ago. He is currently at large and might possibly be armed. There are no leads yet to his whereabouts except for a possible encounter with an upstate farmer."

"Where are you driving to, do you know?" he asks. "We're going upstate to a place where you can stay for awhile. It's a small cabin that my parents have owned for years. My Dad uses it for fishing trips once or twice a year. It's a neat little place, just perfect for us to get away together."

He reaches over and puts his hand under her sundress and squeezes her tan thigh. "I need you bad honey. It's been so long since we made love. I want to lock into your body and soul."

"We'll be there in an hour or so. Meanwhile try to relax will you, you're making me feel really horny." She puts her hand high on his leg. Parker adjusts the seat to a reclining position and closes his eyes as Stephanie continues on.

That night is chilly and Parker looks into the hardwood fire as the wood pops inside the stone fireplace. Parker and Stephanie share a cigarette before making-out in the orange flow of the firelight. They remove their clothes and snuggle underneath a soft down comforter while lying on the thick fur animal rug. They explore each other's bodies, passionately caressing and making wild love into the moonless night while a million Catskill stars twinkle in the velvet sky above the small cabin.

Meanwhile, back in the suburbs, a Private Detective sits behind a large desk in an office with an old style glass door with JOHN MATLIND – SURVEILLANCE AND RECOVERY painted across it. Matlind speaks with his secretary, Julie, about the scene at the prison. "He was right there Julie, about three inches from my face. I just caught a glimpse of him when a flashlight moved across the room. It was like a weird scene from a horror movie. There was definitely something eerie about that whole situation. I also saw a big shadow up in a high corner of the wall when a temporary beam went on. I looked around for Parker who was gone, when I looked back, the shadow had disappeared too."

"It's too bad you couldn't have grabbed him," she replies.

"It happened like that!," Matlind snaps his fingers.

"The thing with the lights threw everyone out of whack. They'll probably catch him in a matter of days. He's like a stray dog, running scared. He is probably all alone and if he goes to his family, they'll nail him quick"

"What a fluke for the power to fail just at that time. It's like a show from the old 'Twilight Zone'. The odds are one in a million." Julie muses.

"You got that right. The whole episode had an unreal feel to it, spooky… kind of supernatural. It's so clear in my mind, especially when I sleep."

"Still think he's innocent?" she asks.

"I'm still leaning that way," replies Matlind. "What came in on Recovery," he asks his secretary.

"Well we have two chalices that were stolen from St. Rocco's, a priceless thoroughbred named 'Fugitive's Way', and a statue of a seated sage that was lifted from a museum on Long Island; plus a backlog of cases that we have to go through and review." Matlind says, "We'll get to that tomorrow," as he reads the horoscope. "When's your birthday Jule'?"

"I'm an Aquarius, John."

"Oh, the humanitarian," he comments.

"Yeah right, that's me, a champion of humankind," she laughs. "What's your sign boss?"

"I was born in early November, I'm a Scorpio."

"Ever sting anyone?" Julie asks. To which her boss replies, "Only when I have to."

Stephanie and Parker leave the upstate cabin, locking the door behind them. Stephanie gazes skyward saying, "Look at all those sparrows."

"They're not birds Steph', they're bats; always in the sky at sundown and dawn."

"Just like vampires," she says.

"Right… just like us," Parker quips. He looks down noticing an injured sparrow. Walking over to the bird, he pulls out a white handkerchief and wraps it in the cloth carefully, setting it aside beneath the porch.

They get into the car and drive slowly down the old country road in the direction of the main highway. High above, the masses of bats merge, darkening the sky as they make their ascent into the realm of the nocturnal, hunting for barns and stables where livestock and horses will quench their thirst for fresh blood.

Parker and Stephanie listen to the radio and make small talk while driving back downstate. After being on the road for two hours they pull up in a parking lot across the street from the bureau of records.

"What are we doing here Parker, this is the courthouse?"

"I've got some business to attend to. I want you to drop me off and go back to your house and get your laptop; then meet me at this spot in one hour. Can you do that?"

"But why are we here, Parker?"

"I need to get some critical information, Steph."

"How are you going to get in there?"

"The way I was taught in sleep-away camp, by an expert locksmith named Lloyd. Now don't worry, just be back on time OK?"

"Sure," she says while hugging him. Then she plants a big kiss on Parker's open mouth. After Steph leaves, Parker accesses the building with a set of lock picks and proceeds to steal the records of his trial containing the jurors profiles and information. He quietly exits the building and waits for his girlfriend, who shows up a half-hour late.

"What took you so long?", he asks as they drive away. Stephanie tells him that the police had been to her house earlier in the day because a Detective left his card in the front door. Her parents aren't due back until tomorrow night so everything is cool for now. Parker expresses a worried look on his face. "You weren't followed, were you?"

"No, don't worry," assures Stephanie. "I was very careful about that. There was a note on the back of the card to call Det. Lawrence and come down to the Precinct the day after tomorrow."

"Don't go, it's a trap; they'll make you tell, they have ways to trick and confuse you," Parker says angrily.

"I have to go in there with a good story; otherwise they'll think something's going on. The laptop is in that bag on the back seat, along with some granola bars." Parker jumps over into the back and begins to put his master plan in motion as Stephanie drives the car back upstate to their hideaway cabin in the Catskill region.

The next morning Parker listens to the news on the radio as he drinks coffee and reads yesterday's newspaper while Stephanie cooks up some bacon and eggs. She puts out a plate of home-fries and a stack of toast for her fugitive man. He has begun to smoke menthol cigarettes and has grown his hair long and added a mustache.

"Listen to this: here's a story on the Jurors from my trial and what a tough decision they had making this conviction. Give me a break, will ya'?"

"Everyone was surprised by that verdict; they thought that you would beat it because of your scholastic background and clean record," Stephanie reasons. "I beat the 'chair' though, didn't I? And now they will all be receiving a special surprise," Parker says coldly.

"What does that mean, Parker?" she asks naively.

"It means, my dear, that I'm going to have a little fun of my own with these famous jurors who put me in that electric chair. I look forward to teaching them how to play the Zodiac game, where your astrological sign denotes your destiny."

"What are you talking about Parker?"

"Payback!! Those sons of bitches put me through an ordeal that ruined my life and reputation. You think I'm going to let that slide? No way; now I am the judge and jury. I'm the high-exalted marionette master… I am the executioner now," he firmly decrees. Stephanie is scared by this side of Parker and tells him, "The main reason I'm helping you, besides the fact that I love you, is that I believe in your innocence in the murder that you were charged with, but the way you're talking now…"

"Yeah, what about it," he breaks in.

"Well maybe you should give yourself up," Stephanie says quietly.

Parker gets mad and replies, "Are you losing your freaking mind or what! Besides, even if I wanted to, I couldn't now. I made a deal in return for my freedom. The time is near to begin to carry out my part of the agreement."

"With who, Parker?" asks Stephanie bluntly. "…With the reaper of lost souls."

"You're telling me that you are going to kill the members of the jury?"

"That's right sweetheart, just the way they tried to kill me. Only difference is that they're not going to get away, like I did." He grabs her arm and she pulls away.

"I'm leaving," she says, "I don't want any part of this madness."

"Try to understand," he counters, "I had very little choice in the matter."

She grabs her bag and opens the door of the cabin with tears in her eyes.

"Go bitch," Parker yells. "I don't care, but you better not rat me out to the cops, or you'll be on the list too. You hear me Stephanie? Don't interfere with my business." She slams the door then drives away crying as she heads towards the Interstate.

Parker opens the juror's files. He notices that their dates of birth are spread out. Three of them are on the cusp though, so he rolls them into the next sign to balance things out. He comes up with a different sign for each juror. "This is working out better than I imagined!" he exclaims as the pieces of his horoscope puzzle fall into place. After reading through the information carefully, he walks over to the television set and turns it on. Only a few channels are available up here. He switches around and a test pattern comes up on the screen. Parker sits back on the cushioned Adirondack chair and begins to focus on the image that he had become accustomed to in jail. He watches, transfixed by the moving shadow in the world beyond the glass as a gust of wind extinguishes the two candles on the stone mantle. Parker falls into a deep slumber as the moon shines full outside of the cabin window. The astrologer sleeps for three hours, waking up at 2:00 a.m..

He reaches for his files, drawing out the name of the jury foreman first. It was Howard George Crenna; born on April 3rd, 1945 at St. Francis Hospital in the Bronx at 2:00 a.m. EST, current address is 14 Dowling St. Yonkers, New York.

"He's an Aries, like me, with Capricorn rising, moon in Sagittarius and Scorpio mid-heaven. He will be perfect for the first victim. I'll hitch-hike or steal a car; whatever I have to do to get to Yonkers to begin to pay back my debt. The jury foreman first. Is this perfect or what?!" Parker exclaims to himself.

On the following day, Stephanie's mother, Janice, answers a knock on their front door. She opens it to find two policemen standing there with a search warrant. The taller one introduces himself as Det. Ray Lawrence, telling her, "We'd like to take a look inside ma'am. We have reason to believe that Parker Wilsone is somewhere in this area."

"I assure you that young man is most certainly not hiding in my house. I wouldn't have it, and my daughter knows it."

"I'm sure you're right," the detective replies. "This is just a routine search. May we come in?"

At this point Stephanie's father, Joseph, enters the room from the kitchen holding an unopened beer in his hand.

"What's going on Janice?" he asks her. The mother turns to him stating, "They're looking for Parker, Joe."

"He's not here! My daughter is going down to the precinct tomorrow, isn't that enough for you people?"

Detective Lawrence asks, "Where's Stephanie now?" to which her mother replies, "She is out for the night to see a movie with her girlfriends."

The patrolman in uniform with Lawrence presents the warrant to search stating that they won't be too long. Then they go about the business of checking closets and crawl spaces with their long black flashlights which are capable of cracking some-one's head open with one shot. The search is in vain as the fugitive Parker Wilsone is nowhere to be found.

After thanking the family for their co-operation, the Police leave the house and continue the task of finding Parker.

In another part of New York a Greyhound bus pulls into Yonkers Terminal. Parker is the last passenger to get off the coach; he begins to walk through town. Stopping at a video game room, the fugitive kills a half-hour or so. He is nervous; this will be the first juror. Sitting on a park bench he reads the newspaper, trying to blend in. He gets up and walks over to the small convenience store. Parker goes in and purchases a bottle of water and a pack of Marlboro menthols, which he opens outside, then lights one up. While he's standing there a black Dodge Ramcharger pulls up and parks. The driver, dressed like a general contractor, gets out and goes in the store, leaving the engine running. Parker stares at the hood ornament which is a large chrome ram's head. He walks around the big pickup and enters on the passenger side, then slides over behind the wheel. Bang!, he throws it in reverse, backs up fast then shifts into drive, burning rubber as he leaves the scene with the stolen vehicle.

Cruising in the vicinity of the intended victim's house Parker familiarizes himself with the surrounding neighborhood. He drives by the jury foreman's house and seeing a light on and a parked car in the driveway he continues on to the local gas station. An old-timer comes out to the pump.

"What'll it be son?"

"Fill her up Pop and fill this liter bottle too."

The attendant says, "I can put gas in your truck, but we're not allowed to give any fuel out in a bottle, it's against the law."

"Well, I'm in a bind," Parker begins to bullshit the man. My grandma's car has run out of gas and she's stuck on the shoulder about three miles down the road. I told that poor old woman that I'd be right back with it."

"Now that you put it that way, I guess it is kind of an emergency, so to speak."

Parker says, "Oh man, that's great; I knew you'd understand. Hell, I'll fill the jug myself." He gets out of the truck with the large glass bottle. The worried attendant tells him, "Just don't let the Law see you with that or tell 'um where you got it, 'K?"

"Hey, no problem Gramps, got you covered." Parker continues to humor the elderly attendant, "I don't want to jeopardize your job now."

"That'll be $19 for everything."

"Here's $20, have coffee on me."

"Hey, thanks pardner," the old man beams from the $1 tip he's received.

"No, *thank* you," Parker says as he shakes the old fellow's hand. The confident fugitive gives the 'thumb's up' sign as he rolls out of the gas station. The old attendant renders a weak wave of his hand. Parker heads down the road toward his destination. Twenty minutes later he turns the corner onto Dowling Street and cruises past #14, a small pale green house located on a quiet block. Parker makes a wide u-turn in the 'cul de sac' then comes back down to park on the street near the house. The car is not in the driveway; he waits for his prey to arrive home while he savors the special blend of coffee in his plastic mug. An hour passes and night falls. Finally, Parker sees a small pair of headlights cut through the night at the other end of the street. He watches nervously as the small foreign car pulls in. Parker has already doused the entire perimeter of the medium sized house. There he creates a fuse made out of gasoline that will allow him enough time to run to the front of the house and jump in the truck. Listening by the living room window, Parker hears the shower go on in the ground floor bathroom. Producing a fresh butane lighter from his pocket, a wicked flame is struck in the darkness behind the house of the man who read the guilty verdict that fateful day in the court room. The gas fuse is ignited—the Horror Scope hunt has now begun. The fire spreads quickly at the base of the wooden shingle house. Parker makes a dash for the truck with his adrenaline pumping at the max. He jumps into the driver's seat but doesn't start it up. He just sits in the shadows watching the flames spread. The old wooden house goes up like a tinderbox. Then Crenna breaks out through the front door wearing a water-soaked bathrobe and holding a small towel across his face. He stumbles off the curb and into the street. Crenna turns screaming as the bright lights of the Ram Charger are thrown on just an instant before the truck is intentionally driven into him. The critically injured man manages to hold on to the large chrome hood ornament, the proud, majestic Ram in his final moments. Somehow, his eyes and Parker's meet for a few seconds during his demise and there is, for a fleeting instance, a realization of sorts; an understanding of reprisal and of duty and consequence. Crenna falls to the street passing beneath the vehicle of death as Parker shuts off his lights and floors the gas pedal, promptly disappearing into the night at the end of the street while behind him, climbing flames greedily devour the house and life of the first juror, and Aries… the sign of the Ram and the element of cardinal fire.

Inside the Police Station Detective Lawrence questions Stephanie while another Detective looks on. The girl feels uncomfortable in the Interrogation Room especially since she's not being truthful about Parker Wilsone. Lawrence knows he can break her but he chooses to go easy.

"Come on Stephanie, you're a nice girl; why don't you level with us about your boyfriend."

"He's not my boyfriend, OK? I'm seeing someone else," she lies.

"Who would that be, Miss?" the other Detective quickly asks. "I don't want to drag him into this whole mess, if you don't mind."

Detective Lawrence moves his chair closer to Stephanie. He leans forward, speaking in a quiet voice, "If you know Parker's whereabouts and refuse to tell us, it's the same as harboring a criminal. Should Wilsone commit any crime while he's on the loose, that will make you a direct accessory to the fact. I personally don't think that you want to be in that position. Do you have anything that you want to say, Charlie?" he cues the other detective.

"Understand what he's saying Stephanie? You don't want to do time honey, 'cause them girls in the lockup just love fresh pussycats like you."

"You're trying to scare me and I don't like it," she yells. "I've got nothing more to say without my attorney present, it's my right as a citizen."

"I hope it's not the same one that Parker used," laughs Lawrence along with the other cop.

"All you cops are the same, you know that?" The frustrated girl blurts out; to which Det. Lawrence says charmingly, "Not really sweetheart, I'm one of the nice ones. Right Charlie, tell her."

A Police Sergeant knocks on the door, then hands in a sheet of paper with a computer printout on it. He gives the page to Lawrence saying, "I think you ought to see this Chief." The Sergeant then quietly closes the door. The detective reads the paper silently, then looks up at the girl. "Before we let you go home Miss, I just want to let you know that a man up in Yonkers had his house torched and when he ran outside he was deliberately run down by a stolen pickup truck that quickly disappeared."

"So what does that have to do with me?" she questions Lawrence.

"It just so happens that the deceased was the foreman of the jury that convicted Parker Wilsone. We're talking arson and homicide here. Is there something you'd like to tell us now, Stephanie?"

"No there's not. I've got to go. All this stuff you're saying has nothing to do with me. Goodbye." She gets up and walks to the door of the Interrogation Room. The two detectives are seated facing her.

"Oh by the way Stephanie," Lawrence says. She turns asking, "Yes."

"You don't wear denial well."

"Goodbye," she says as she's walking out the door. Lawrence has the final word as he caps the meeting with, "Good luck."

Parker walks down the street on a sunny afternoon. He stops in front of a pawn shop and checks out the goods in the window. After a few minutes Parker decides to walk in and see the rest of the merchandise. There is something for everyone here. Guitars hang on the wall above other musical instruments. Some rifles and expensive power tools rest quietly, waiting to be recycled back into society's stream of action. But it is the brass-trimmed glass case that displays various types of knives from around the globe that catches Parker Wilsone's eye; the small Spanish sword style dagger stands out.

"What kind of weapon is this?" Parker asks the clerk.

"Oh, the one with the long shiny blade. That's a Spanish 'muleta'; used by the matadors to finish the beast. Sometimes they only get one good chance to make the kill."

"It's an interesting dagger," Parker confides. The clerk replies, "A very traditional weapon, one with a history of honor."

"How much is it?"

"It's rare," the pawnbroker says, "but I'll sell it to you for fifty bucks."

Parker pulls out a wad of crumpled mixed bills. And without saying a word he puts three bills on the ledge in front of the pay window. The clerk takes the currency and pushes the *muleta*, wrapped in a brown paper bag with colored rubber bands. Parker thanks him and leaves the pawnshop with the shiny dagger in his possession.

Three days later he follows the next juror, a Taurus, into the Museum of Modern Art. Vincent Noray strolls through the massive galleries as he views exhibits by famous artists. Noray finally enters a section that is dedicated to the works of Pablo Picasso. The former juror slows down his pace in order to appreciate the genius that is Picasso. He is an Art connoisseur and a collector on a small scale. Hearing footsteps on the marble staircase causes Noray to turn around. Parker Wilsone slowly ascends the steps to the upper gallery. Noray glances at him, then looks back at a large rectangular black and white piece titled, *Guernica*, which depicts the large head of a bull standing over the abstract forms of men, one of which lies on the floor holding a broken knife blade in his hand. It is a very violent looking picture that was done in 1937. Parker walks over to the same picture and begins to show mild signs of being in a relaxed trance. Vincent Noray looks over to him nonchalantly as he comments, "Sometimes violence can have a strange sense of beauty."

"Yes Vincent, it definitely can."

"Do I know you? How do you know my name?" Noray says with a nervous tinge in his voice.

"You knew me… my name is Parker!"

"What?!" says the confused man.

Wilsone kicks Noray hard in the lower stomach, bending him over forward. Parker then raises the matador's dagger and thrusts the weapon into the back of Vincent Noray, the second juror to meet his death at the hands of this satanic avenger. The fatally wounded Noray falls to the floor beneath the Picasso painting; his hand clutches his back, then tries to reach the short sword protruding from it, in vain. The dying man utters, "Oh my God, oh God help me," as Parker slowly shakes his head from side to side while he watches the blood leave the body of his prey. He walks closer to his victim, and then says, "Goodbye brave Taurus, you have served me well." Parker then turns and walks briskly away. Two women enter the gallery and spot the body on the floor. They scream out, causing Parker to run to a fire exit door and disappear down the stairwell.

Matlind drops the newspaper on his desk. The headline reads ART GALLERY HOMICIDE along with a front-page story and photograph of the covered body below the Picasso painting. Matlind pours a cup of coffee then sits down and opens the newspaper to the Astrology page, where the daily horoscopes are listed. The *Post* starts the signs with Virgo to Libra, Scorpio, Sagittarius, etc… Matlind then asks his secretary if she's bought a paper that morning. To which she holds up the *Daily News*. Matlind gets up and walks over to her desk; he can't help but notice Julie's shapely legs as he approaches her for the paper. Turning to the window, the private investigator thumbs through the pages in the light from the Venetian blinds. "These forecasts start with Aries," Matlind states. "So does *Newsday*," Julie adds. "That's two out of three for Aries. It's not the beginning of the year like Capricorn but it is the Spring sign." The secretary comments that the jury foreman, who was recently murdered, was born in early April. Matlind turns to the Obituaries where he sees the second victim's birth date as May 2nd under the sign of Taurus, the Bull. He counts off on his fingers, "Fire, earth, air, water. If that was the case, then Gemini is next. I need the names, addresses and birth dates of all the jurors in the Parker Wilsone case *pronto*." His secretary picks up the phone, "Right away John!" Matlind sits back down at his desk and continues to read the Astrology forecasts. "There's got to be a pattern," he quietly confides in himself.

Meanwhile in a Manhattan TV studio, the buzz is on about the murders. Make-up artists prepare Mr. & Mrs. Wilsone for the news cameras. Their photographs have been in the daily papers and the public's interest in the case is growing. The newscaster introduces the couple in their fifties as the parents of Parker Wilsone whose disappearance on the night of his execution still remains a mystery to the authorities. "We have with us tonight the parents of Parker, who would like to say a few words to him if he's out there listening."

Janice Wilsone speaks first. "If you're listening son, I want you to know that we miss you very, very much… and urge you to turn yourself in right away to the proper Authorities." His father Frank says, "It's for your own good Parker; believe us, do it before it's too late. We don't want anything bad to happen to you son." Mrs. Wilsone adds, "Please son, do what is right, we're all praying for you." The local newsman sums it up with: "Parker Wilsone always claimed his innocence after his murder conviction. His bizarre escape from the electric chair on the night of the blackout is still remembered by many as the first big story to break the next morning after power had been restored." The camera then shifts to another newscaster, an attractive female who reports, "In the news today, a cold blooded stabbing at the Metropolitan Museum of Art… details when we return."

Somewhere in a large department store, a young man stares at the forty television sets on the stacked shelves of the audio/video section. He seems to feel a greater distance than ever from his parents and society, now that he has become a professional fugitive. One who is on a mission of destruction and answers only to a higher authority; a force of evil and grim demise. After viewing the newscast on the multiple screens, Parker Wilsone quietly walks away, heading toward the escalator.

Back in Matlind's office, he's going over the juror's birth dates and finding that, although some are on the cusp of two signs, there is a distinct order that could be arranged as the twelve different signs. John notes that the jury foreman was the first; he was an Aries, the Spring sign. He was the victim of fire, Aries being the cardinal fire sign, and vehicular manslaughter, carried out to precision using a stolen Ram Charger, the March/April sign is represented by the ram. Next to go was Noray, a Taurus, who was slain with a European dagger designed and used for killing bulls in the ring, while viewing a Picasso at the Met; the picture also showed a bull and a man with a knife in him, it is titled *GUERNICA*. The sign that follows is Gemini, the twins. Referencing the jury list, Matlind picks up the phone and dials in Cynthia Wexler's number. He gets a busy signal and hangs up. Her sister, a fraternal twin, is on the phone with an old friend from out of town. Clutching the telephone between her cheek and shoulder she proceeds to fill her blender with various protein powders and fruit juices. Samantha is a bit of a health nut who works out in their small home gym daily and has developed quite a shapely body through her disciplined efforts. She hangs up the phone which rings again in two minutes. This time her sister, Cindy, answers it upstairs as she is getting dressed for a date with her boyfriend. The Private Detective on the telephone makes her aware of the possible danger that Parker Wilsone might present, advising her to be cautious when she goes out to work or when shopping. Matlind mentions the possible pattern of the jury offing but says that it's too early to tell yet if his theory is correct. She promises to come to his office sometime next week when she has off from work. Downstairs, Samantha loads the blender with yogurt and a banana. She places the lid on securely and presses the 'chop' button; the banana abruptly disappears from the surface of the liquid, it's whirring noise fills the kitchen, hiding the footsteps of the stranger in the house as his work boots quietly make their way up to the second floor. The 'grind' button on the blender is then pressed increasing the noise and rpms. The stranger, dressed in dungarees and a flannel shirt makes his way down the long hall to Cynthia's room where she is sitting in a white slip putting on nail polish at her make-up table with two hinged antique mirrors.

Downstairs, the 'blend' button is pushed, magnifying the sound once again. The old glass doorknob to Cynthia's bedroom slowly turns. She is unaware of the intruder as she admires her freshly painted nails. He gently pulls on a white silk belt that slides out of the loops of a teal bathrobe hanging on a closet door. The intruder walks behind her suddenly appearing in the dressing table mirrors. The woman, completely caught off guard, recognizes her assailant just as the silk sash passes between her eyes and the reflection and wraps, at first softly, around her neck. Downstairs, Samantha presses the blenders 'liquefy' button as Parker's hands cross behind the woman's head, administering a quick twist into a death grip. As Cindy reaches for her throat, she knocks over the bright red nail polish that streams across the dressing table, dripping off the edge and onto her lacy white slip. Parker Wilsone looks down on his victim and mutters, "Cancer is next." He then descends the staircase under the cover of the blender's noise, but as he reaches the door the mixer stops. He hears footsteps coming from the kitchen so he ducks into the small hallway closet. Samantha walks over to the front door and opens it looking up and down the street. She returns to the kitchen area and pours out a glass of the healthy concoction. "Cindy, the shake is ready… Cindy." Samantha walks up the stairs to her sister's room to find her lying on the hardwood floor in a pool of red nail polish. She screams as the front door is quietly closed downstairs.

Two days later John Matlind enters the Police Precinct and goes to the main desk.

"Where can I find Detective Lawrence? I'm Matlind, a private investigator."

"What is it in reference to?" the desk Sergeant asks. "The Parker Wilsone case," the private eye replies. Just then Lawrence comes walking down the hall to his office. The Sarge motions to Matlind, "That's him now," pointing to the Police detective. "Thanks," John says, then walks over and introduces himself to the officer, who seems to put him off but allows Matlind ten minutes in his busy day. They enter a private office where Lawrence sits behind the desk.

"Close the door Matlind and have a seat. Now what's this all about?"

"It's regarding the Parker Wilsone case, Astrology and serial murder. He's out to kill the jurors from his trial systematically, according to their birth dates and signs of the Zodiac."

"Where did you get this theory from, a comic book?"

"There's nothing funny about the three jurors that have been silenced since his bizarre escape. I was there that night, in the execution room, when he vanished into thin air. The kid is deranged and using a definite pattern in exterminating them."

"Nice theory Matlind, but I don't buy it," Lawrence says wryly.

"Well the Aries and the Taurus have already bought it and just last night the Wexler woman was found strangled in her bedroom to the horror of her twin sister."

"It still doesn't look like any distinctive pattern yet, as I can see. We'll have to wait and watch how it plays out. The jurors have all been alerted to the situation."

"Alright, see how many more get killed. I'm willing to bet that the sign of Cancer is next and then the Leo, Virgo, Libra, Scorpio, and so on, right down the line. You want names Lawrence, I'll give you names!"

"It's an interesting theory Johnny, but it just doesn't have enough weight yet. I've got a meeting in five minutes with the Chief. Good luck though, thanks for your interest."

"Thanks for your time… think about what I said."

"Will do Matlind," says Lawrence, holding the door open for the private investigator. He watches him walk down the corridor then closes the office door and sits in his chair rubbing the sides of his head with his hands.

The winds of early summer travel across miles of the pre-season empty beaches. Claudine Zarro has already rented a small bungalow in an attempt to get away for a while and relax. She has brought half a dozen Clive Cussler paperbacks along with Stephen King's current novel. She has walked about fifty feet from her cottage to a spot in the dunes where she likes to sunbathe in her brief two piece. A lone watcher across the grassy dunes, at a higher elevation, keeps an eye on the attractive blonde through an old spyglass purchased from a local antique store. She lays out a large colored towel on a secluded section of the closed beach, nestled in the rolling dunes. The stranger slowly makes his way along the sandy terrain, closing in on the girl with each step. She rests on her back with headphones on and a small radio next to her; eyes closed, she appears to be napping in the late afternoon sun. Suddenly a shadow comes between her form and the brightness above. Her eyelids flutter and she quickly sits upright. The man steps back and the bright rays of the sun cause her to squint as she strains to make out the mysterious figure standing over her.

"Remember me, Claudine?" the stranger quietly asks. Shading her face with her hand she nervously blurts out, "No, what do you want here, this is a private beach, you'd better leave."

"Come on, take a good look, bathing beauty." Claudine gets up and walks a few steps out of the line of the sun. She looks at him now and realization shows on her face.

"Coming back to you now?" asks Parker menacingly. The pretty blonde grabs her towel and radio and attempts to leave the area but Parker grabs hold of her wrists.

"Let me go or I'll yell for help!"

"Go ahead, bitch, yell and the wind will steal your voice," he says. She opens her mouth and screams but Parker grabs her, covering Claudine's nose and mouth with a chloroform soaked rag. Upon inhaling, the close to naked woman begins to succumb to the potent liquid. Her assailant turns Claudine around, holding her body tightly to his as she melts in his arms. Parker looks around scanning the vacant beach before picking her up and carrying the unconscious girl down along the shore-line in the direction of the rock jetty. An elderly couple, out for a stroll see the boy carrying her down the beach. The old man looks at his wife saying, "Remember when we were that young?"

"Indeed I do," she replies, "It's as if it were yesterday." Her husband of forty-five years smiles as he looks out at the sea, "Hmm... yesterday."

Day becomes night as the moon rises slowly above the girl tied spread eagle to spikes driven in the crevices of the rocks. The spray of the incoming water occasionally wets Claudine's body, clad only in a two piece bathing suit. She opens her eyes into the night, tightening up in her awareness of the bonds that hold her captive.

"Have a nice nap?" Parker asks.

"What the hell is going on you sick bastard!"

"It's almost a cloudless sky tonight; just the way I planned it for you, my little moon child." He leans over to kiss her and she twists her head, turning away from him. "Have it your way Claudine. You know, I always had kind of a thing for you, but it was impossible to do anything about it under those circumstances, in the courtroom and all. Now things have changed though and maybe we can spend some quality time together. You know, get to know each other on a different level." Tears begin to flow from her irritated eyes, "I held out until the end on that guilty verdict— 'til the end. The rest of the jury pressured me into it, I swear Parker!" Her captor snaps out a stiletto knife. She looks at him with eyes and mouth wide open. He slowly brings the blade near her neck as she whimpers and braces for the worst. He makes a quick cut right then, separating the front of her shoulder straps from the top of her suit.

"Don't cut me," she pleads.

"Your demise must be astrologically correct," he lays up against her side, gently kissing her neck.

"I'll do anything you want, just let me go… I'll never tell anyone about this."

"Yeah right Claudine. I'm afraid it's a lot more complicated than that honey. I made a deal with a heavyweight in the Underworld, and I'm not talking about the mob. But I am forced to follow through now; right to the end. The night tide will be in soon and it's time for me to leave you now."

"I don't deserve this Parker, you know that!" she screams at him as he stands up, hideously back-lit by the moon.

"No more than I deserved what I got for a crime I never committed. Think about it… I was right at death's door with my hand on the knob."

"Don't leave me here in the cold," she begs; "I don't want to drown."

"You probably won't drown, this is where the crabs come to roost," Parker says as he slips away into the thick fog bank rolling in along the beach. The doomed girl can faintly hear his fading voice saying, "Goodbye Claudine, it's too bad it had to be like this… it's too bad, goodbye sweet moon child." He jogs down the beach, disappearing into the night as hundreds of crabs begin to surface on the rocks where Claudine is tied. They cover her body as she screams in vain on the isolated beach beyond the dunes. They pinch her with their large claws as her life's blood is slowly drained, streaming down the jagged rock jetty and into the sea waters of the incoming night tide that is drawn by the skull-faced moon above. Parker continues to run through the night winds until he stops, out of breath and vomits violently at the end of the sand dunes.

Matlind reads the daily newspaper's account of the bizarre murder of Claudine Zarro on the shoreline of Long Island. He says to his secretary, "Well, there's our juror, sign of Cancer, devoured by an army of crabs on a moonlit night. Which means that Mr. Jacobs is next, being under the sign of Leo. Maybe Parker will burn his house down too." Someone enters the front door but Matlind can't see them from back in his office. The secretary points the prospective client to Matlind's partially opened door. John has his head buried in the paper when she walks in asking, "Are you John Matlind?" he replies, "Yes I am," without looking. "What can I do for you?" he asks nonchalantly looking up at the attractive brunette dressed in black. "I'm Samantha, Cynthia's sister. And I want to hire you to bring her killer to justice," she says, as her voice becomes filled with emotion. The Private Eye can't believe how outrageously beautiful Samantha is with her perfect hourglass figure. He thinks to himself, 'this babe is hotter than a three alarm fire in a salsa factory.'

"Excuse me, but you don't resemble your sister much," John notes. "That's because we're fraternal, not identical twins. I've just come from her funeral and felt that I had to stop by and talk to you."

"Well I'm glad that you did," says Matlind. "Won't you have a seat Samantha?" She sits down and crosses her legs, asking for a light for her long thin cigarette. Matlind uses the small table lighter, and then sips his coffee. "Would you care for something to drink Samantha?

"No I'm fine," she replies. "Actually, I would but it's too early in the day." Matlind looks across his desk in mild disbelief at this woman in mourning, all wrapped up in black silk and nylon from head to toe and wearing a hat with veil from the 1950's. Sure he'll take the case; it's right up his alley, besides he's already looking forward to seeing her again. The addition of this client also gives him a solid interest in this bizarre crime of jury eradication.

"I would like to see the low-life who did this be locked up and executed so that other future victims might be spared," Samantha Wexler tells Matlind.

"I've already been researching the twisted plot; that's why I contacted your sister, to warn her."

"I live on Meadowrue Lane. Would it be helpful to come by and see Cindy's room?" she asks him. "If you would be alright with that," he replies. "That's no problem," she says, "Please call me tomorrow, I've got to go." He shakes her gloved hand then watches her walk out of his office. Sitting back down behind his desk the Private Detective thinks about the way she looked, in her mourning dress.

"You're not falling for her already, are you, I mean you just met her John," Matlind's secretary asks. "I refuse to answer that." His face changes to a contented smile.

"She looks like that famous pin-up model in the 50's," he says.

"Do you mean Grable?" the secretary asks. "No," John replies, "the other Betty".

Things were quiet until a dark blue Riviera pulled into a three car garage attached to a large suburban home one hot night in August. A middle-aged man exits the car loosening his tie as he walks into the house. He is Edward Jacobs, a former member of the Parker Wilsone jury. His wife is away this weekend, visiting her parents in Martha's Vineyard. Ed's got the whole house to himself. The successful businessman mixes a drink then drops down on the plush couch. Thumbing the remote, he turns on the big screen television then gets up and walks across the cool ceramic tile floor to the more than adequate bathroom where he relieves himself. When he returns to the spacious room he finds the television set shut off. Ed looks around for the clicker but cannot seem to locate it. He senses that he's not alone in the house. His instincts prove to be right when a voice speaks from behind him to say, "Lost your clicker Mr. Jacobs?" Ed realizes immediately who it is. He turns to see Parker Wilsone standing in his living room.

"I know who you are; the Police are looking all over for you," Jacobs says as he inches his way to a large antique desk. He tries to be casual but he is nervous as hell. Parker senses this just as a shark in the water near his victim can feel certain vibrations. Jacobs pulls the top drawer open and reaches in frantically. Parker kicks the drawer shut, holding it closed with the bottom of his foot. A gunshot from a small caliber weapon is fired inside of the drawer. Parker hits Ed on the shoulder blade with a fire iron, causing the tall man to yell as he rips his damaged hand out of the smoke-filled drawer. "What do you want with me… I can't change the past." He stumbles back, writhing in pain.

"Then how about the future?" Parker quips. "Sit down Jacobs, we're going to play a little game of Chess at this fine table that you have been thoughtful enough to provide." Parker holds his two fists out in front. "Black or white?" asks Parker. Ed picks the hand holding the white piece. "That means you have first move Ed… but you realize I'll probably have the last. But I'll have to be careful 'cause I heard you're a good player."

"What do you want Wilsone?"

"I want a game," says Parker, raising his voice. "The stakes of which are your body and soul." Thunder rumbles somewhere in the distance as the Zodiac merchant of death takes his seat across from his soon-to-be-next victim. One hour later, the game is over.

The midnight blue Buick sedan slowly moves down the dark driveway with the headlights off. On the other side, in the front of the house, Jacobs hangs suspended from a wrought iron archway with a stone lion statue sitting on either side at the base. He actually had won the Chess game, which infuriated Parker who struck the ex-juror repeatedly with the fire iron upon being placed in 'checkmate.' Now the victim hangs in the rain of the passing storm as his killer drives his dark sedan into the night, having been bludgeoned to death and suffered extreme blunt force trauma. Inside of the car, Parker has a smoke as he states to himself, "The sign of Leo has been brought to justice." The crazed and bitter youth pushes his mad ambition onward.

Detective Lawrence drinks his morning coffee from a styrofoam cup as he reads the startling headline regarding Ed Jacobs. "Get that Private Eye, Matlind on the phone Charlie."

"Right away Chief." Charlie replies.

He quickly dials him up. Julie answers the phone in the private detective's office. "Recovery, may I help you?"

"Yes", says Charlie, "Please have Mr. Matlind call Detective Lawrence at the Twelfth Precinct. Thank you."

"I'll give him the message," says Julie.

"Let's let him sit for awhile," Matlind smiles to his secretary. Back at the Police Station, Detective Lawrence turns the pages of the morning newspaper. "There might be something to this Astrology bullshit after all. Say Charlie, what sign are you?"

"Get the hell out of here," is the old cop's reply.

Matlind's secretary contacts Stephanie and manages to set up a meeting with the Private Eye. The former girlfriend of Parker Wilsone shows up an hour late. Matlind takes her out of the office for a walk down Main Street where they duck into a little neighborhood coffee shop called 'Portofino.' Taking a quiet table in the back section they drink house blends as the detective gets to find out more about the prodigy known as Parker.

"He's a genius Mr. Matlind," Stephanie gushes.

"Call me John, Steph. It's a lot easier. I understand he's also a formidable Chess Master."

"That's right…John. Chess and Astrology are his key fields."

"A deadly combination for an avenging serial killer, don't you think?"

"We still don't know for sure if Parker's involved in these jury murders," she says half-heartedly.

"A guy named Dylan once said, 'You don't need a weather-man to know which way the wind's blowin'. And that's pretty much the way I feel about this one."

"That's not fair Matlind; the law says innocent until proven otherwise, you know that," she counters, in defense of her former boyfriend.

"You're speaking from your heart… not your head Stephanie. I'm on your side in this case. Work with me to bring him in safely before it's too late," he confides. "I was there the night of the intended execution. Just before your boyfriend did his disappearing act I saw him for about six seconds; he was standing as close as I am to you. I just stared in disbelief; it was like I was paralyzed."

"So what do you want with me?" she asks innocently.

"I want you to bait the trap and help draw him in so that he can be captured and taken off the street for the good of every one, including, and most of all, himself."

"That's a pretty rotten thing to do, setting him up and all. I don't think that I can be a part of that… I'm not into it Mr. Matlind; sorry but I've got to go." As she stands up to leave, the Detective takes his last shot.

"Are you into standing by while he methodically kills the rest of the Jury? Help me Stephanie, and we'll be saving Parker from himself."

"We don't know for sure that he's actually killed these jurors. I'll think about what you said, but there's no guarantee that he'll even call."

"We need to set up a trace and trap," says Matlind.

As they leave the coffee shop both are unaware that someone is watching them. A newspaper with another homicide headline is cautiously lowered to reveal Parker's sinister smile as the pair drive away in Matlind's car.

That night, Stephanie's telephone rings just as she gets out of the shower. Wrapping a small towel around her wet body, she picks up to hear Parker on the line saying, "Hello Steph, you miss me? I'll tell ya', I'm sure missing you."

"Where are you?" she asks in a concerned tone. He tells her that he's not too far from her house but can't risk being seen there. She hears him depositing change in the coin phone.

"Can't be too careful nowadays."

"I want to see you Parker," says Stephanie. "It's been a really long time since we've been together."

"You seem really anxious; wouldn't be trying to set me up for something, would you Steph?"

"You're sounding a little paranoid Parker, are you alright? You still miss me, don't you?"

"Sure I do, but not just now, I'm too hot and there's still a lot of work to be done… know what I mean Stephanie?"

"You're not responsible for the dead jury members, are you Parker?"

"You know they say that the two signs most likely to commit murder are Aries, through impulse, and Scorpio through pre-meditation—and I've got Sun in Aries with Moon in Scorpio, isn't that cool?"

"You've really changed since we were together. It's like I don't even know you any more… maybe I never did; you're like a split personality and it scares me, Parker."

"The reason I'm different now is because one night in the city I happened to turn the wrong corner, and that changed my whole goddamned life. And regarding those jurors, yes, I did what I had to do." His voice becomes more menacing as he tells her, "I saw you with that private eye, bitch. I know you're trying to set me up, but it's not going to work Stephanie, I've got you pegged." He hangs up on her. She puts the phone down on its stand and lets the tears flow from her eyes.

As Matlind does research on a case at his desk his secretary opens a letter addressed to her boss with a strange seal on the back of the envelope that reads:

> *To Mr. Matlind — Zero are your chances of ever finding me, did you think you really could in such a big city? This Master of the Zodiac strikes when least expected; he is everywhere, yet nowhere at all. He cannot be detected. But when at last we shall meet, my presence will electrify, as those lost souls from the jury go flowing, rolling by…*
>
> *Parker*

After he finishes reading the spooky epistle, Matlind looks up at his secretary. "He must have seen Stephanie and I together the other day. That girl's the key to catching him. Parker's paranoid delusions of grandeur have him believing that he's invincible but sooner or later that genius is going to slip and lose his own life over this insane horror scope vendetta."

"Do you think he'll be apprehended before he obliterates the entire jury, John?"

"I hate to say it Julie but I think his revenge will be complete; he might even finish off the Judge before it's all over and done with—which reminds me that I've got a meeting with the remaining jurors at Judge Morton's estate on this coming Friday night."

"That's the thirteenth," says Julie, looking at her calendar."

"Figures," Matlind replies as he raises his shoulders in a brief gesture.

The next several days are uneventful, but on Friday the phones keep ringing in Matlind's office. He leaves just before sundown on his way to the Judge's mansion out in the Hamptons where the remaining seven jurors are seated around a huge mahogany table in the Great Room, soaking up the ambiance of the international artifacts as the fire roars beneath the large mantle. Judge Morton re-enters the rooms saying, "Please feel free to have another drink as you relax; oh, and thank you all for coming to this meeting on such short notice. It's been two years now since we've last seen each other and I am extremely concerned with the events that have taken place since Parker Wilsone's mysterious escape."

"Do you think there's a good chance of Parker being apprehended soon your Honor?" asks Denise Pacet.

"I feel confident that he will be once again brought to justice and shall face his intended demise. Let's wait until Mr. Matlind arrives to further discuss that. He's been following this case since day one and has many views to offer regarding it."

"Do you expect him soon?" asks Ryan Mitchell, "I have an important appointment to make later on this evening in Sag Harbor."

"Maybe this Zodiac nut got to the Private Eye! You never know in this crazy world," crows Billy O'Connor, a bartender from Bayville.

"That's hardly amusing, William," adds the pretty Adrian Wright.

Margaret Sinclair then asks, "Are we going to be given Police protection, Judge?"

Avoiding her question Morton looks out of the window at the circling headlights. "A car has just pulled around in the driveway; it's probably Matlind now," His Honor announces. As the next few minutes pass the guests act uneasy as they wait for the Private Eye to appear. The butler finally shows Matlind, accompanied by an attractive brunette, into the vaulted ceiling, heavily beamed Library section of the Great Room where the remaining members of the jury wait.

"Ah good, Mr. Matlind, and friend, everyone is anxiously awaiting your presence." As Matlind enters the room he slowly and carefully looks at each person without speaking. The Judge and Jury exchange glances back and forth, obviously off-balanced by this Private Investigator's silence. Denise Pacet, a stewardess for a major airline breaks the ice with, "Well, aren't we supposed to ask you questions about this madman that's running loose in our city?"

Waiting to speak, Matlind finally says, "I want you all to ask yourselves some questions."

"Such as?" chimes in Adrian Wright.

Matlind holds the chair for his guest to sit down then he follows. He speaks quietly and directly to all present. "Such as, where are you most vulnerable in your daily routine? When is it easiest for someone to get to you."

"You sound pretty serious," states Billy O'Connor nervously.

"Dead serious!" Matlind replies. "He's sharp and calculating… not to be underestimated. If the killer is Parker he might have once been innocent but has now, through some twist of fate, morphed into a cold-blooded killer. He lives for the act of revenge against those who condemned him to death for a crime that he claims he never committed."

The senior citizen of the group asks, "Who's next Mr. Matlind?"

"If Wilsone's pattern holds true, it will be… the sign of… Virgo!"

Upon hearing this Margaret Sinclair, the youngest of the group, shudders as she clutches her lace handkerchief. Standing up, the Private Eye begins to slowly walk around the tables as he introduces his new client to those present. "I've taken the liberty tonight to bring Ms. Samantha Wexler here to meet you all. Her sister, Cynthia, became a victim just recently. It happened in the afternoon while Samantha was in the house, downstairs. You never know; stay aware as you go through your daily routine." Then Matlind continues reading from his 3x5 index cards that he produces from his sport coat pocket. "And then Libra follows Virgo," as he looks over at Ryan Mitchell, "and then the sign of Scorpio," angle on the raven haired Denise Pacet. He turns to Bill O'Connor, "next is Sagittarius, followed by Capricorn as Terrance Anderson finishes his drink. Then the humanitarian, Aquarius," Adrian Wright lowers her eyes. "And finally Pisces." Amelia Gilbert covers her heart with both hands while looking around at the others. The elderly woman is mildly terrified.

"Are you sure of all of this Mr. Matlind?" asks Judge Morton, showing concern for the jurors. "95% your Honor. I hate to be the bearer of bad news but this is the way the situation has taken shape. I've been following it since Parker's arrest. All the signs are there, cleverly dispatched in order." Matlind walks across the ample

Persian rug then stops abruptly, telling the former jurors, "Now that you have been made aware of the facts, it is up to you to take as many precautionary measures as possible."

"Why can't the cops find this son of a bitch?" questions Billy O'Connor. "He can't be that smart. The Police aren't trying hard enough to locate this nut-job serial killer. Shit, they're probably afraid of him too."

"Not true," Matlind counters. "There's a Detective Lawrence attached to this case, who is set on bringing in Parker Wilsone soon. It's a little murky though as we're not sure if he's involved in all of them. Parker has got an uncanny sixth sense... like he's being directed by some unseen mega-force."

Margaret Sinclair states, "I demand some sort of Police protection. My life is in immediate danger because of the incompetent Authorities; it's my right as a citizen."

"Yes Miss Sinclair, you'll get one officer assigned to be with you, inside of your apartment. But only you... until something new develops. As for the rest of you, you're on your own for awhile, good luck. Please take one of these business cards with my office number on it. Stay alert and don't hesitate to call me if you feel it necessary. Thank you all for showing up tonight. Both myself and the Judge feel that this meeting will afford you an advantage."

"Now that the business at hand is finished please relax and stay for a cocktail," says the good Judge, making everyone feel at home. Some of the jurors say their good-byes and leave while others stay and loosen up a bit from the intense discussion. They all knew Samantha's twin sister Cindy and were very fond of her. Samantha's being there helps the closure process for everyone. Judge

Morton and John Matlind stand and converse near the large fish tank. "When is your birthday Judge?" asks the Detective. "I'm a Pisces Mr. Matlind," Morton replies. "The last sign of the Zodiac," Matlind adds. The two men sip their drinks as they stare into the water of the large tropical fish tank.

The next morning Matlind reads the *New York Post* police blotter in his office, as his loyal secretary, Julie, fields the incoming phone calls and faxes. "So how was the meeting last night John?" she asks inquisitively. "It went well Julie; it was both necessary and productive, I brought Samantha along."

"She's nice, I like her. Are you two getting to know each other?"

"Well, as best as we can under the circumstances, but I would like to take her out somewhere special; you know, beyond the scope of business."

Julie thinks for a minute then asks her boss, "Have you ever heard of the Eve of All Saints Ball?"

"No, I haven't," the Detective confesses.

"Well the tickets are close to impossible to get and I managed to procure a pair this year, but Wayne, my boyfriend has to fly out to a business meeting in Atlanta the day before so I may be able to hook you and Sam up… interested John?"

"What is this now, a Ball?" he asks. "Yes," she replies, "It's held every year at a different location; this time it will be hosted at an estate in Old Brookville. Only one hundred and fifty people are invited at two hundred dollars per couple, interested?"

"Yes," he says, "I take it's a costume party, right?" Matlind asks, becoming more intrigued by the moment.

"Of sorts," she comments, "Oh, it's a masquerade alright but the dress code is restricted."

"In what way Julie?" he inquires. "All of the males must wear black tie tuxedos… and all of the women must dress as French maids."

"Really," the Private Eye responds, now definitely intrigued by the whole concept of this Halloween party.

"Yes," says his secretary, "That's why they call it the 'French Maid's Ball'."

At this, Matlind picks up the phone and dials Samantha's number. "What about your professional client relationship," she needles him.

"That's exactly what I'm hoping to develop here Julie." After a brief conversation Matlind hands his secretary two crisp $100 bills. "The tickets are safe at home; I'll bring them in for you tomorrow," she says as she takes the money, "You won't be sorry John, plus you'll get to see her and seventy-five women dressed to the 'nines'. You'll also need face masks, you know, like the Lone Ranger wore."

"Right," he responds quickly. "That is going to be an outrageous night," he quips.

"That's for sure," adds Julie.

Young Margaret Sinclair had come to New York from St. Louis about five years ago when she was twenty. As time passed she became very comfortable in the big city. While working as a waitress she pursued her passion in the career of acting. She played a few parts in small off-Broadway productions and had just recently read for an independent film project. Tonight, a Police Officer named Charlie Sommers sits in her kitchen playing solitaire as he listens to the baseball game on the radio. The woman he is playing guard dog for relaxes on the couch in an adjacent room watching an old sitcom re-run. Charlie drinks a cup of coffee midway through the Yankee/Red Sock game as Marge looks into the kitchen. "I'm going to sleep early tonight," she says. "Please help yourself to anything in the fridge or cupboard if you get hungry Charlie. 'See you in the morning." Smiling, she bids him goodnight.

"Goodnight Miss Sinclair… sleep well," replies the cop.

Marge Sinclair opens her bedroom window to let her cat in for the night. Looking down to the street beyond the old-fashioned fire escape she notices a dark sedan parked in the alley across the way, but doesn't think anything of it as she turns off the night-table lamp and removes her clothing, changing into a large size tee shirt. Her black cat settles down for the night on her comforter. She pulls the covers over her and nestles into the pillow.

An hour and a half later a street light by her building is shot out by a pellet gun. Another hour passes and a figure dressed in black, wearing a navy blue ski mask slowly climbs up the fire escape to the third floor window of the room where Marge Sinclair sleeps peacefully. Entering the room through the unlocked window, the dark figure crouches, waiting for any sounds as his eyes become acclimated to the darkness. There is no night light in the small bedroom but the intruder sees the reflection of the shards of moonbeams interrupted by the partially drawn blinds in the pet cat's eyes. Marge's guardian angel, Charlie has sacked out on the couch about an hour ago and is occasionally snoring. The black garbed figure rises to a standing position as he removes a pillow case with the symbol for the astrological sign Virgo from his pocket then quietly places a pillow from a chair in the room into it. High in the sky outside, night clouds cover the waning moon, adding to the clandestine scenario of darkness inside the room. In an instant the perpetrator is on top of the girl with the pillow covering her face. She wakes up unable to breathe. The stranger in the night holds her down as Miss Sinclair silently struggles for her life; her black cat scratches at the door but Charlie just could not stay awake to set her free. Suddenly Margaret tightens up, then goes limp, drained of life and being. The gloved hands of her killer remove the pillow from her face; then removes his ski mask. Leaning over her in the dark he kisses and caresses the young woman as the black cat returns to the night through the fire escape window. After briefly possessing his prey, Parker exits through the same window escaping into the all-consuming nocturne.

Three weeks later another relatively young juror pulls up to the massive building that houses the Supreme Court complex on his ten speed bike. He locks the bicycle in the rack at the base of the seventy odd steps then carries a thick leather satchel up to the huge stone landing beneath the sequoia-like columns. Lunchtime has ended two hours ago and a few people pass through the metal revolving doors. Parker Wilsone emerges from behind one of the mammoth pillars reading a super-hero comic book. Fifteen minutes later the delivery has been made to one of the many legal offices and Ry Mitchell exits the building through the brass trimmed revolving door. Stepping out into the bright sunlight he heads toward the top step and is suddenly attacked and pushed by Parker who runs down the infinite number of stairs, passing Ryan whose body bounces uncontrollably from the gathered momentum. The courier breaks many major bones on the way down the never-ending levels to the sidewalk where he crashes, head on into the base of a ten foot statue of a blindfolded woman holding a sword in one hand and a set of scales in the other. Now at the bottom, Parker Wilsone quickly cuts the small chain lock on Ryan's bicycle and rides away through the heavy Manhattan traffic before any of the bystanders can comprehend what's happened. Guided by the hand of the Devil, Parker has killed the messenger, the Juror who was under the sign of Libra. His plans are now forming for the demise of the Scorpio, Denis Pacet, as the small crowd of onlookers gathers near the fallen man.

Detective Lawrence stands in his office with three other Detectives and a dozen Patrolmen. His voice is filled with a sense of urgency, now that another former juror has met their fate, "I want every available man on this case twenty-four hours a day. Do you understand me?" he questions his men.

"Yes sir," one Patrolman assures, "We'll find this son of a bitch… guaranteed!"

"Nothing's guaranteed Mallary; we've got to track this killer down and bring him in dead or alive," Det. Jameson says, "He's got to screw up sooner or later, the odds are against him now, I don't give a shit about how smart he is."

"I want daily reports on all the remaining jurors," says Lawrence, "and overtime for the officers who work on the case, we got to nail this head-case before another juror ends up in a box."

"What about the Mayor's budget?" someone asks.

"To hell with the budget," shouts the angry head Detective. "He's the one who led the Crackdown on Crime campaign. The

Mayor pushed for Wilsone's conviction to make his point, but now when the backwash comes in he doesn't want any part of it and he's slowly turned into a lame-ass Liberal. A policy that was originally gung-ho has given way to a caretaker administration." Jameson tells the group, "We still haven't located the Pacet broad. She might have left the state because of the heat on her, we don't know." Lawrence makes it clear, "Eh, if the woman takes it on herself to leave town she's on her own. That's it. If the dame would have cooperated with us we could have set Wilsone up and nailed him this time. It doesn't matter now. Double up surveillance on the Bartender, what's his name?" One of the Patrolmen answers, "It's Billy O'Connor."

"If Parker can't find Pacet, he might go after this kid who's the next juror in line." Detective Lawrence shakes his head, "Who'd have believed this Astrology bullshit was for real. Watch O'Connor like a hawk. Station a couple of plainclothesmen in the bar...soft drinks only; we've got to lock this screwball up before he does any more damage."

The rest of the men leave the office. Det. Lawrence looks at the collection of newspaper headlines on the small table next to his desk. He picks some up and violently rips them in half, then throws them into the wastepaper basket.

Meanwhile across town, Denise Pacet is frantically packing her suitcase while her closest girlfriend looks on.

"You're better off taking my cat to your apartment than coming here to feed him. This madman might just mistake you for me. I canceled all my flights for the next three weeks and I'm not telling anyone where I'll be, including you," says Denise as she hastens to evacuate her small studio apartment.

"That's fine, just call me though and let me know you're alright, OK," her concerned friend Carol reminds her. "They're bound to catch him soon," she says hopefully.

"That's bullshit Carol, the cops can't even keep up with him; and yours truly just happens to be next on the Astrology Hit Parade."

"Maybe you'd be better off working on a long flight," Carol speculates.

"Yeah," says Denise, "like Australia or something. I've thought about that but what if he manages to put a bomb aboard a flight. Hundreds of innocent people would be wiped out; I'm doing what I feel is best Carol."

"I guess you're right Denise," her loyal friend Carol confides.

"If you don't hear from me, I might have Roy call you. We're going to an elite private Halloween Ball together; then we'll be on a secret getaway vacation for maybe a month," spills Denise.

"I thought you were going alone?" asks Carol innocently.

"Are you serious? I need some kind of protection; I'm on Parker's hit list. Roy and I have been talking about getting away together for a long time anyway, and this is our chance."

"Just be safe, I don't want anything to happen to my best friend," says Carol to Denise, after which they hug each other, never knowing that their worried embrace will be their final contact in this world.

Denise takes the elevator down to the parking garage where she heads towards her car at the other end of the underground facility. Looking over her shoulder occasionally as she walks across the concrete floor pulling a small piece of luggage on wheels and carrying an overnight case she feels another presence in the garage. She speeds up her steps in order to get to the car sooner. Suddenly, one of the custodians steps out from behind a concrete partition wall, almost causing a collision between the two. Denise is startled and drops her luggage, holding her hands over her mouth in terror.

"I'm sorry I scared you Miss," says the worker. He bends down and picks up her things for her.

"No… thank you, it was my own fault," Denise says, realizing that the man works there. "It'll be alright." She walks to her car and opens the trunk, placing the luggage inside then closing it firmly. She gets into the driver's seat and starts the car, checks her make-up in the mirror, lights up a cigarette, turns on the radio, looks back over the front seat to make sure that no one is hiding back there, then opens the electric window, throws out the cigarette and drives out of the parking garage. The discarded lit cigarette with lipstick on the filter burns slowly, smoking on the polished concrete floor. A hand reaches down and picks up the butt taking a drag and French inhaling the smoke, then flicking the cigarette away.

A dark Buick sedan with New Jersey stolen tags on it cruises out of the garage and pulls up to Denise's car at the light. The stewardess looks over at the dark sedan with the tinted windows and says to herself, "Calm down girl, don't be so damn paranoid." The traffic light changes and she takes off fast, heading toward the outskirts of town. The mysterious car drops back in traffic but continues to follow her.

John Matlind sits in his office that night, lit only by a small desk lamp as he talks to Samantha Wexler about the French Maid's Ball. After they hang up, Matlind goes back to his book on power

Astrology. Not five minutes passes when the Detective sees a shadow pass through the unlocked front door and into the small vestibule. He quickly shuts off the lamp and drops to the floor drawing out a small caliber Dickson Detective revolver. He moves quietly across the carpet, taking cover behind a cubicle partition as he sees the shadow of a cap-wearing stranger opening the inner-office door. The silhouette emerges and Matlind cocks the revolver; the intruder freezes in his tracks.

"Tell me who you are right now of I'll shoot you in a very painful and uncomfortable place, capish?"

"Don't shoot Matlind, it's me, Kevin Lincoln, don't shoot me."

Matlind rises and turns on the light switch. "What are you doing snooping around at night like this Kevin?"

"I came by to see you and found the door open and the lights off. I thought maybe you left and forgot to lock it, so I came in to see what was going on, Holmes."

"What did you come to see me about Kev, and this better be good, bro'."

"It is. You know I wouldn't bother you with any bullshit. I got the name of this Chinese dude who's a Master of Oriental Astrology, he's even communicated with the dead, you dig?"

"Yeah, I dig," says Matlind, "Go on."

"Straight business, Holmes. They call the man Dr. Chang, the dude's got the Astro trip down tight." Kevin hands Matlind a matchbook with the phone number handwritten on it.

"What makes you think this Sage can help us find Parker Wilsone?"

"Now I don't know if the man can do all that but I figured it was worth a shot to check the dude out."

"OK," John says to Kevin Lincoln, "Thanks for the lead, Holmes." The twenty-year-old, who sometimes helps Matlind with anything from moving furniture to getting coffee from Portofino to assisting on a Recovery case, bids the Detective goodbye and disappears in the cold night winds.

They're going to the Halloween Ball in Samantha's car. Matlind waits by the window while nursing a Chivas Regal on the rocks. As soon as he finishes the drink and walks into the bathroom, headlights appear in his driveway. Minutes pass and Samantha gets out and walks around the silver Monte Carlo and gets in on the passenger side. She presses the horn again and John locks his front door and walks to the car. He gets into the driver's seat and looks over at Samantha, who leans in and plants one on his lips. She sits back in her seat wearing a thin expensive raincoat over her dress. Matlind casually notices her black heels with the leather bows.

Her legs are so sweet that he's starting to get a cavity, just looking at them.

"I'm excited," she says.

"*You're* excited?" replies the Detective. They drive off into the Eve of All Saints night, on their way to the 'French Maid's Ball'.

The roads to Old Brookville are foggy that night. Matlind drives cautiously until they reach the entrance gates to the mansion, which is set back at the end of an extremely long driveway. When they arrive beneath the portico entrance a valet advises them to don their masks before leaving the car; which they do and then enter the large front door where they hand their invitations to the masked ticket taker who signals them through the Gothic archway to the cocktail hour room. Aside from the butlers doing service, every man is dressed in a tuxedo and every woman is wearing a French maid's outfit; a pretty incredible sight, and the night is still young. After checking their coats, John and Samantha have a drink and begin to loosen up a bit. Expensive appetizers such as super jumbo shrimp and miniature lamb chops grace the service platters along with an extravagant sushi bar. Roving cocktail waitresses furnish the open bar assortment of alcoholic beverages to the masked crowd. The music is just starting to filter in as more of the elite guests arrive in their high end automobiles. There are hot, attractive women everywhere as the couples enter the Great Room where the DJ controls the sound and the lights. The bass is pumping and the alcohol is flowing at the exclusive French Maid's Ball.

A butler with a close-cropped beard and his hair tied back in a ponytail offers drinks from his silver tray to Denise Pacet and her boyfriend. Everyone is having a great time at the Ball. The music is cranked up and the special effects lighting is putting everyone in the "party zone". Sherman Whalen IV, heir to the drugstore fortune, circulates among the revelers with a beautiful French maid on each arm, as Matlind and Samantha get lost in the celebration of the evening spirit. They dance great together and begin to really warm up on the slow ones. Her hourglass figure is hard to miss; she's the 'cat's meow'.

Leaving her beau for awhile, Denise goes to the powder room where two other women are fixing their hair and makeup, even though they will be wearing masks when they once again return to the Great Room. Denise is left alone as they exit the Ladies Room. Her mask removed, she touches up her lipstick, then smoothes out her nylons. Hearing the door she waits for the next person to come into the narrow room. Instead of a woman, one of the butlers enters and offers her the last glass on his tray. Thinking that it is unusual, she still takes the glass of white Zin and begins to drink from it. The butler puts the tray down and turns the lock on the inside of the door. Then he removes his mask and looks deeply into the girl's eyes. The raven-haired beauty is slightly drunk and stands up as he comes forward, closing their distance. She starts to feel uneasy, but it is too late. He smiles, showing a white set of snap-on vampire teeth; an actual denture with the canines filled with the deadly venom of the scorpion. She tries to pass him and get to the door but he grabs her and pulls her into his arms. Turning his head to the side he bites into her soft neck, activating the liquid housed in the fangs. She struggles and he puts his leg between hers to hold her still, his hands are all over her as she squirms and moans. After a long half-minute the vampire butler steps back and removes the apparatus from his mouth. Denise has sat down on a cushy antique chair and is slowly slipping into unconsciousness. Parker Wilsone puts his mask back on, unlocks the door, and quietly leaves the powder room. Denise slumps and falls to the marble floor unconscious. Parker passes her boyfriend on the long winding staircase as he makes his way down to the Great Room, where the guests are really rockin' now. "Some party, huh?" says the impostor butler to Roy. He then crosses the dance floor, where he pauses next to Matlind, who is having a drink with some of the other guests. Their eyes behind the masks meet briefly before he turns and angles his way out of the gyrating Halloween crowd. It causes the Private Detective to pause for a minute within the conversation; an eerie example of the past floods his mind.

Upstairs, Roy is looking for his date. He checks the series of small bedrooms and day rooms but has no luck. One of the guests in her twenties comes up the stairs and walks into the powder room, closing the door behind her. As Roy passes by he hears her scream, then throws open the door to see the girl standing near Denise Pacet's lifeless body, spread out across the cold floor. Just as Roy goes to his fiancee and kneels by her side, a voice at the doorway says authoritatively, "Don't touch her; this is a Police matter now." Matlind enters the small room and looks over the body noting that Denise, whose mask had been removed, has two distinct punctures on her neck. He kneels down, bending over her, and smells the wounds.

"We'll take it from here Matlind," says Detective Lawrence, as Det. Jameson and two Patrolmen who accompanied them seal off the mansion. They've never been on a case where they have encountered over fifty women dressed as French maids in the same room; it's quite an experience for them; one that could easily drive them to distraction. All the guests are told to remove their masks. One of the cops looks over at the other one and says, "There's more cheesecake in this room than a Paris pastry factory".

The other cop says, "I roger that Halahan, we're talking some serious French benefits".

"Another juror joins the list," says Matlind to Lawrence.

"We tried to get in touch with her, but she skipped out on us; there was nothing we could do Matlind," Det. Lawrence tells him.

"It's a shame… she was a vibrant girl," Matlind responds; "if she only would have cooperated with us, we might have captured him"

"Do you think it was Parker for sure?" asks the Police Detective.

"I'd bet my lungs on it," says the Private Eye. Samantha comes over to Matlind's side.

"How are you tonight Ms. Wexler?", asks Lawrence. "I'm a bit shaken up and would like to be escorted home," the attractive brunette tells Matlind. "It's in their hands now John, there's nothing more that you can do here."

"Tell Jameson that I said you can leave Matlind. Be careful on your way out, they're still searching the grounds," cautions Lawrence.

"Knowing Parker, he's long gone. It's time to focus on Billy O'Connor now," cites Matlind.

"We've already got that covered Johnny," says Det. Lawrence.

"I hope so, because after November 23rd it's going to be open season on him. Let's go Samantha, the party's over," says John.

After getting their coats they leave the mansion, waiting in front for the valet to bring up their car. The silver Monte pulls up and Samantha slides in behind the wheel as Matlind tips the kid a five dollar bill. They listen to smooth jazz as the Monte Carlo heads back to Samantha's house where they spend the night together in Cynthia's bedroom and consummate their new relationship. In the morning light, both tuxedo and maid's outfit are found strewn across the soft carpet. Samantha, awakens next to John with a strong sense of closure and fulfillment. She looks over at him, sleeping soundly, his arm outside the covers bearing an old Army tattoo of an eagle. Samantha sits at the dressing table with the dual mirrors. While combing out her long brown hair she thinks about Cindy and what she went through at the end.

Samantha would never be satisfied until Parker Wilsone has met his intended fate, but she knows the chances of that are small... she hopes that she is wrong.

The two Plainclothes men assigned to guard Billy O'Connor sit at a small table in the Bayville Bar & Grill. The ship's wheel clock on the wall reads close to one a.m. now, almost closing time. Det. Jameson says, "Hey Billy, we're going to pack it in for tonight. Looks like everything's going to be cool, OK?"

"Sure, that's no problem, go ahead. Thanks a lot guys, I appreciate you keepin' an eye out for me."

"You closing up soon?" Jameson asks. "In about twenty minutes," says Billy, "one for the road?", he asks.

"Sure," says Jameson's partner, "we'll have a couple of shooters." They raise the shot glasses ceremoniously and then it's down the hatch.

"See you tomorrow," says Jameson. "Take care of yourself, kid."

"Not a problem, I can handle it," says O'Connor.

The two Detectives leave the bar and Billy goes to the small bathroom in the back, near the little kitchen. When the bartender returns there is some guy with a beard and long hair sitting at the bar eating peanuts.

"Eh sorry, we're closed pal," says Billy to the stranger. "The door was open dude, so I walked in."

"Well OK... have a brew on the house," says Billy as he draws a mug of beer from the tap, then slides the full glass down the mahogany bar to the untimely stranger who catches the handle and then raises the brew saying, "To your health," silently laughing to himself.

"Where'd you get that bruise on your forehead, in a fight?" questions Billy.

"Walked into a door," the customer says matter-of-factly.

"You know, I think I've seen you someplace… ever been in here before?", Billy pushes the question. He comes from around the bar saying, "I'd better lock this door before someone else comes in looking for a late night drink."

"Good idea Billy," says the man at the bar.

"How do you know my name dude, I thought you said you'd never been in here before."

"I was at your Birthday Party last year. That was December 9th right, you're a Sagittarius," removing his sunglasses the stranger looks Billy O'Connor dead in the eyes, "the Archer." Billy goes back behind the bar, heading towards his riot gun.

"Wait a minute…" Billy half-heartedly says as Parker Wilsone brings up a crossbow pistol from inside his long over-coat and rests the weapon on the bar rail. Billy steps back then grabs a double barrel shotgun from underneath the bar. The bartender points the riot gun at Parker's chest. The fugitive pulls the trigger on the crossbow sending out a short pointed arrow that passes through the bartender's chest lodging itself in the mirrored wall behind the bar. The shotgun explodes one round that goes straight up, shattering the glasses hanging from the overhead rack. Billy spins around holding his wound with one hand and the shotgun in the other. A second round of gun-shot fires and the mirror behind the bar is completely demolished as O'Connor falls to the floor, holding the spent weapon in his dying hand. The harsh winds of the early winter sweep through the wide open doorway. The music has stopped and Parker has once again disappeared into the waiting arms of the night.

Matlind and Kevin Lincoln cruise up the property of Dr. Chang's country estate on Long Island. After parking in the circular driveway they walk to the large mahogany front door. The exterior screen panel is made of heavy iron in the pattern of a spider's web. Kevin strikes the steel ring through the dragon's nose, that is the front door knocker, twice. A muscular Asian man opens the heavy door.

"Dr. Chang?", asks Matlind.

"No sir, I am Leung. Are you Mr. Matlind and Lincoln."

"That's us bro'," assures Kevin.

"Please enter," says Leung.

They walk into a big foyer with a wine red Oriental carpet on the wall. The floor is expensive bamboo tongue and groove. An intricately carved teakwood border runs across the top of the walls' perimeter and outside corners.

They enter an anteroom where four high backed chairs surround a black oak table. Kevin and Matlind are told to take a seat by Leung, who disappears immediately thereafter. The small high-hat lights in the ceiling are then dimmed down for the entrance of Dr. Chang. A soft sounding gong is heard just above the soothing ancient Mandarin music; the next thing they know, he's sitting in the chair between them.

"Good evening, gentlemen, Mr. Kevin Lincoln and Detective Matlind; so good of you to come to my country home for assistance in this mysterious chain of events. I can only say that I will try my best to be of help to you."

"Thank you for having us on such short notice, Doctor," Matlind says. Kevin asks about the empty chair and if someone else is expected.

"Perhaps the spirit of Parker will occupy that chair this evening," Chang replies.

"Shall we begin," urges Matlind.

"Yes… first clear your minds," councils the Chinese doctor. "Then place your hands, palms down with your fingers spread wide, at a shoulder's width. Close your eyes gently and place your tongue at the roof of your mouth; breath only through your nose while slowing your breathing down to a minimum." Kevin looks over at Matlind and then all three close their eyes. Silence fills the room, finally broken by the altered voice of Dr. Chang saying, "Take your place among us Parker, for you are the true reaper of the Zodiac fields. You are the harvester of souls of a dark and evil mandate. Join us with your migrating field of consciousness, Parker Wilsone; link with those persons here present."

The room goes silent once again. A long five minutes of silence passes, then Chang speaks quietly, just above a whisper, "I can see in my mind's eye a vision of inter-winding patterns of double parallel lines… there is also a monk who gleans in the high wheat fields… large, slow turning circles passing by… angled stripes… and a strong light, maybe lightning… also a distant light… very faint… fading." Chang snaps out of it and just sits there for awhile as John and

Kevin cautiously open their eyes. Dr. Chang turns up the dimmer switch and the three sit there without moving an inch. "I hope that I have been of some help to you Mr. Matlind," says Dr. Chang.

"It's all very interesting Doctor, but a little too cryptic right now," the Private Eye replies. Dr. Chang points out the faint out-line of two hands on the table in front of the empty seat. Matlind seems to think that they were artificially created somehow. When Leung comes into the room to see them out, the Detective asks Chang's bodyguard to place his hands in the outlines. Leung complies and his hands are bigger then the outlines on the table. Satisfied, Matlind and Lincoln leave the house of Dr. Chang and drive back through the hollows of the rolling North Shore back roads.

"What did you think, Holmes?" asks Kevin of Matlind. "There's something definitely there… but it's vague and clandestine. Images are a dime a dozen. The question is, what do they mean collectively."

"And the hands?"

"That could have been manufactured, cause if it wasn't, then it means that Parker's spirit was in attendance."

"That's weird shit Boss," says Kevin.

"This case gets weirder every time I turn around Kevin; you know what I mean, Holmes?" says Matlind, turning his head.

"I hear ya," Lincoln confirms.

They both think about the session with Dr. Chang in silence as the sudden rain streams down the windshield.

Clarence Anderson drives along the slick road in the rain. He's on his way to the Brew Haus to meet with friends for dinner. He drives a dark gray Lincoln Continental along Francis Lewis Boulevard. A midnight blue Buick follows Anderson as he turns on to a less populated roadway, continuing on, into the rainy night. He's had a bad right front tire for awhile. It was plugged but also had a slow leak that was never fixed. The wheel hits a sharp rut in the road and the tire begins to falter. Mr. Anderson is then forced to pull over. What a lucky break for Parker; this is going to make things a lot easier than he had planned. Parker slows down and passes him on the side of the road, then drives down about twenty yards, turns around and heads back. He stops across the way from Anderson who is getting soaked while looking in his trunk for a scissor jack.

"Need a hand Mister?", Parker asks innocently. "Thanks for stopping," the unsuspecting Anderson replies. "It looks like my spare is shot too. Can I bum a ride to a gas station?"

"Don't see why not. Hop in and get out of the rain," Parker coaxes Anderson. The Buick then drives off in the downpour. Once on the road, Parker turns up the heat. Wilsone takes a back road to an old station that he says he knows, but it doesn't really exist. The car finally pulls up on the side of the road by an archaic cemetery.

"Where are we?", asks the former juror nervously. "Why are we here? I want to go to a gas station NOW!"

"Shut up," yells Parker, pulling out a Luger pistol, "And get out of the car!"

"What the hell is going on here? You're not going to get away with this… is it money you want?", rants the captured man sternly.

"Walk!", yells the crazed Astrologer as the rain begins to pick up again. They move in staggered steps between the tombstones in the height of the passing storm until Parker signals Anderson to stop in his tracks. He sticks a shovel in the earth. "Dig," he commands his captor.

"I know who you are now. How much money do you want Mr. Wilsone? Ten thou', twenty… you tell me, OK?" He then reaches into his pants pocket and pulls out four hundred dollars. "Here, take this; there's more, plenty more Parker," he says assuredly. Wilsone reaches out and takes the cash; after all, that's how he's been surviving so far; by stealing from his victims, inspired by the shit he learned in the joint when he did his bid. Parker drops a small canvas bag on the wet ground. As he turns back to Anderson, the shovel hits him flat on the shoulder blade; he falls firing a shot on the way down that passes through the captor's leg. Anderson collapses on a downward slope. Parker limps over to him, holding his upper arm. He looks down at the juror, slightly leaning over. Suddenly Anderson catches Parker's foot with his feet and throws the youth down in the mud. He jumps on top of Wilsone and starts continuously punching him in the face. Parker knees him in the groin, causing Anderson to fold. Stumbling to his feet Wilsone grabs the shovel and strikes the juror hard. Anderson drops back on the ground, propped up by an old tombstone. Parker Wilsone reaches into the bag he's been carrying and pulls out the head of a goat! He limps over to the stone and places the goat's head on top of it. Then a step back and points the German pistol at his victim's forehead saying, "Farewell Capricorn, sign of Cardinal Earth. Now ye shall return from whence you came… pop!!" Anderson's facial features freeze in a death glance, as the German luger fires.

The dark Buick drives off into the pouring rain as flashes of lightning illuminate this latest consequence of Parker's soul-selling deal with the Prince of Darkness that eerily manifests itself in Capricorn's demise.

Detective Lawrence calls a special meeting with his cohorts and chews them out for dropping the ball at the Bayville bar and grill.

"Nobody got hurt on my watch Jameson, because I stood there while O'Connor locked up; then watched him drive away in his car. That's when the night's over for you— and only then!" Those in the room remain silent as Det. Lawrence scans them, eye to eye, as he quietly underlines their failure to protect the deceased juror.

The high noon sun's rays filter in through the Venetian blinds on the windows of Matlind's office. He catches up on some paperwork while Julie fields telephone calls. Kevin drops by at 1:00 with lunch and coffees from Portofino. They discuss the case briefly, then Kev leaves on some Recovery business.

"Kevin's thinking of joining the service; the recruiter offered him a good College deal, plus tech school options," John tells Julie.

"You were in the Army right?"

"Yes," the Private Eye answers. "Did you go to tech school John?"

"Yeah, it was called Airborne 101."

"And did they teach you anything?" she asks.

"They taught me how to hit the ground running," he replies.

The phone rings and Matlind picks up the receiver, answering "Recovery." It's Samantha calling. They talk for a bit about where they'll be going out for dinner that night, then it's back to work as the afternoon clouds appear.

Driving a stolen black Jeep, Parker Wilsone enters the East Hampton Library parking lot. Inside of the building another jury member, Librarian Adrian Wright, rolls a metal book cart past the Generalities section and into the Philosophy and Psychology division. It is late and the facility is locked… and Adrian is alone, save for the elderly security guard who is being tied up in his underwear in the basement. Upstairs, Adrian takes her time replacing the newly returned books on the shelves. She moves down the line into the Religion and Mythology section. A book falls from a nearby shelf, startling her. Adrian walks back and bends down to pick it up. She thinks that she hears a slight noise and freezes. While standing there she notes the number 135 on the spine of the text. She slowly turns the book to read the title, "Astrology and Black Magic." She looks around between the lines of the shelves as paranoia sets in. Turning the cart around in the narrow aisle she heads back to the main desk, but stops when the lights suddenly go out. All is quiet in the darkness as the frightened woman hears a whisper in the unlit Library. "Adrian… I've come for you… don't fear me." As Mrs. Wright begins to scream, a hand comes out of the dim surroundings and clamps a thick wad of gauze saturated with chloroform over the Librarian's nose and mouth. She struggles nervously at first, but melts in a matter of thirty seconds and is silently carried away through the dark corridors of Literature.

Parker props her up in the Jeep's passenger seat, strapped in by the safety belts. He drives out to an abandoned barn with a small stone well on the property. When Adrian comes to, she finds herself suspended by a rope from her ankles and hanging half way down in a very deep, still active, stone well. Her mouth is gagged and her eyes are wide open as she struggles in vain to free herself from the madman's bonds. Up above, Parker begins to crank the handle, lowering the poor woman down to her terrible fate, while he speaks in a strange voice:

"Air into water shall mark the eleventh sign. My sweet Aquarius it is time for you to make your unfortunate descent into the final abyss of ultimate darkness where you shall become part of the subterranean and join with those many banished creatures of the Underworld… farewell and so begone my beautiful conquest, Adrian, and so begone." After lowering the eleventh juror to the bottom of the well, Parker looks over the circular stone wall into the blackness thirty feet below. Leaving the rope intact he walks back to the black Jeep that he stole from an iron worker in Wading River and drives onto an old road that takes you out of the boondocks and back on the main thoroughfare.

Three weeks later, the last and oldest juror watches the six o'clock news on her small television screen with her trusty pit bull, lying beside her on a folded blanket. The Newscaster delivers the most recent Zodiac crime developments; "The decomposed body of Adrian Wright, an East Hampton Librarian, was discovered today after a three week search, on deserted farmlands on the East End. Det. Lawrence of the Homicide Division says that the victim had been drowned. The prime suspect in a recent string of murders is the fugitive at large, Parker Wilsone, who escaped execution on the night of the electrical blackout a few years ago. The death of Mrs. Wright leaves only one juror still living from the group of men and women who brought in the 'guilty' verdict in the Simon Watson murder case."

Upon hearing this news, the senior citizen pushes the remote control button to change the channel but it fails to work. Instead, the news program begins to dissolve on the screen and is slowly replaced by an old test pattern. The woman leans back on the couch as she clutches her chest, then fumbles for a bottle of aspirin nearby. Unable to open the childproof bottle under stress, she reaches for her heart medication. Swallowing a couple of pills and spilling water on the front of her house dress she sinks back into the couch. Her dog becomes excited and wets the blanket on the couch. He jumps off and starts barking while running around the coffee table. The strange image of the Grim Reaper begins to form, occupying the screen and beckoning to the confused old woman who has a massive heart attack and collapses. The test pattern returns to the screen as she stares out at the tube with open eyes and a frozen look of horror on her seventy year old face. Her pet pit bull whimpers and paws her body, licking the dead woman's face repeatedly. Her motionless body is not discovered until late the next afternoon when the landlord's wife checks in on Amelia Gilbert. The pit bull runs out the door and down on to the street where he searches frantically for food. The last of the jurors had passed on but Parker Wilsone's deal with Lucifer is technically incomplete since he wasn't directly involved in the termination of the Pisces juror.

The crowd slowly moves up the steps and escalators as a small group scan the timetable board above the ticket booths. Off in a corner stands Parker Wilsone reading the New York Post in Penn Station. He's angry over this new development and thinks out loud to himself, "Shit, who'd ever figure the old lady would kick the bucket like that; it's a good thing I've got a primary substitute in mind. I won't be cheated by this twist of fate. It is truly convenient that His Honor is also born under the sign of Pisces… the Judge will take Miss Amelia's place… perfect," he confides in himself contentedly. Parker rides up on the escalator to the street level then out the doors of the bustling Penn Station. He walks for three blocks to where he parked the stolen Jeep. Stopping abruptly he watches two Patrolmen around the vehicle. Turning around casually he buys a pretzel from a street vendor then promptly gets lost in the crowd, returning to the small basement studio he has been renting for the past two months. After viewing an hour of Judge Wapner on TV, Parker shaves off his beard in a mirror above the kitchen sink. He then confronts his image, staring into the empty eyes that he sees in the reflection until the chimerical vision of the Grim Reaper replaces his own form and Parker becomes one with the Master of his guilty soul. He goes out to the small garden through the sliding door to the back patio where he kneels down by a large rock and gazes up at the waxing perigee moon through the windblown night clouds. The act of self-examination cuts him to the quick. His whole life passes before his eyes as he remembers removing that cursed knife from the fatally wounded Simon Watson's stomach that fateful evening in the alleyway in the city. They never caught the one who did it and Parker had to take the fall. His thoughts turn to Stephanie and all those times they had together. Parker really misses her now and it makes him quite depressed to think about his girl in her skimpy black bikini. He thinks about his parents and his old clients. The fugitive recalls the ten thousand odd Chess games he's played and the struggles and the harshness of being locked up in the joint. This review of his existence is disheartening at best, but he knows what it is that he must do to secure his place in the ledger of eternity.

One week later, on a moonless night, Wilsone steals a dark green Mustang and drives it to the house of Judge Morton. He enters the property from the wooded area near the east side of the mansion. Coming up silently behind a security guard, Parker cracks him in the head with a rock the size of a softball. When the victim falls to the ground Parker steps over him and continues on, seeking his unsuspecting target beyond the amber light of the dim lit windows. When he breaks into the library section of the house he is confronted by the rather large butler whom Parker knocks out with the metal fireplace poker. Nothing is going to stop him or get in his way now; he's too close to completing his deal with the Devil. Parker looks around the room at the mounted animal heads gleaned from exotic safari's and high-end hunting junkets. It appears that the Judge is a regular Frank Buck; a great white hunter, so to speak.

The perpetrator hears someone descending the staircase and grabs the World War II Samurai sword, discarding the scabbard. Holding the sharp blade vertically Parker stands behind a thick velvet puddled drape with the sweat pouring down his brow. He hears someone enter the big room and walk over to an antique roll top desk that is near where he is standing. Judge Morton hears a strange sound behind him. He turns around to see a thick drape been severed by a sword blade from the top to the bottom; then to his horror, Parker Wilsone steps out into the Library, holding the Judge's prized Samurai sword in his hand with an insane smirk on his clean shaven face. He looks around the room at the mounted animal heads on the wall saying, "You're quite a hunter Morton. But this night… you are the hunted. I am here on behalf of these beautiful creatures, who were cut down, murdered in cold blood in their prime for the gratification of annihilation of species in the name of 'sport' hunting."

"If you kill me Parker Wilsone, I'll become your thirteenth victim and that act shall seal your death!"

"Becoming a little superstitious in your old age Judge, but it didn't bother you that my scheduled execution fell on the 13th of the month, on a Friday night! Besides that, I technically did not get to do in that old woman, nature took care of that for me."

"You know you're indirectly responsible for her heart attack Parker; so don't be so heartless," counters Morton as his captor walks over to the gigantic fish tank. Parker speaks as he runs his finger through the water, "This is certainly a fitting collection of fish for a Pisces your Honor. I had planned to do in Miss Amelia before her heart gave out. So now it is you who will take her place as the final victim of the Zodiac Configuration. You should feel honored Judge Morton. This is truly a case of 'last but not least'."

Morton gets up from his armchair saying, "This has gone too far. Give yourself up son, it's a lost cause. The Law is going to catch up with you; it's just a matter of time, and you don't have much of that left."

Parker's head revolves slowly until he makes eye contact with the Judge. He walks over to Morton as he carefully raises the sword up to his shoulder. The Judge freezes as Wilsone speaks, "Now I am the Lord High Executioner and you must prepare to face your execution, the way I faced mine. Remember, 'The Lord is my shepherd, you must pay your debt' … for endangering an innocent man, and sending him on an evil vendetta that has lead him to this room tonight. Do you have any last words, your Honor? Speak now, for your time is dwindling quickly."

"I have some money in my pocket that might change your mind," the Judge baits him. Now Parker always needs money so he asks Morton, "How much are we talking about?"

"About a thousand in cash," Morton tells him. Parker then makes the mistake of telling the Judge, "Let's see it." The Judge reaches into his sport coat pocket, pulling out a Colt Derringer, which he promptly fires at Parker, hitting him in the right shoulder at close range causing Wilsone to step back and curse the tactful Judge Morton who manages to get off the second round before the sword comes down fast, cutting deeply into the point between the neck and shoulder. In shock and bleeding profusely, Morton drops to one knee in front of Parker. The Judge still holds the empty small caliber cowboy gambler's gun as the final stream of smoke exits from the octagonal barrel. His follow-up shot caught Parker on the side of his neck because he moved just in time. Parker's second cut proved to be near fatal; Morton is bleeding like a stuck pig and still kneeling, about to black out. The crazed Astrologer raises the Japanese sword overhead, and then has a flashback to the Day Room in the prison where he served his time before the intended execution. A vision of the TV set with the standard test pattern frozen on the screen fills his mind. Shaking his head quickly, Parker snaps out of it as Morton lowers his eyes. The razor sharp sword blade drops like a thorough guillotine, severing the Judge's head from his Honor's body. Bright red blood gushes from the stump of Morton's neck, spraying Parker's face with a fine red mist that he licks from his lips. The dead Judge's body falls back on the expensive Indian rug; an expression of horror inhibits the distorted facial features of the decapitated head, which Parker drops into the massive fish tank. The aquatic occupants begin to feed off of it immediately. Parker Wilsone pours himself a brandy glass full of Amaretto and raises it in a toast to the murdered Judge Morton. Parker's shoulder feels like it's on fire so he drinks with his left hand, then smashes the crystal glass into the large stone fireplace, signifying completion of the Horror Scope. Parker places a folded white linen napkin beneath his shirt on the gunshot wound to absorb the blood. He walks past the fish tank about ten feet or so then turns and savors the vision of Morton's head submerged in the water. As a final disturbing note of closure, Parker throws the Samurai sword at the large glass tank, shattering it and sending everything inside to the carpeted floor below. Wilsone exits through a leaded glass window as many beautiful expensive fish squirm on the floor around the Judge's decapitated head. A large house cat enters the room.

When Parker hits the driveway he experiences an incredible rush of energy far beyond anything that he's ever felt before. He can feel the blood running through his veins and pumping his overworked heart. Wilsone hears sounds coming from the house as he ducks into the heavily wooded area on the south side of the mansion. He picks up a narrow trail and goes with it for about two miles in the dim light, until the empty road comes into view. Walking toward the lights of a few small stores, Parker stays on the inside of the narrow highway where the night's light is decreased. His shoulder wound is burning like hell, but the boy keeps on going… got to keep moving forward. Approaching a small convenience store he spots three vehicles; a pickup truck, a van and a VW bug, which happens to be running. Parker looks around briefly then jumps in and takes off down the road. It's like driving a big roller skate, but this is not a time for fun. He has completed his deal with the Devil but has lost his soul in the bargain. There is only one thing left that he must do, and that is to see Stephanie one more time. He tunes the radio spasticly as he gets as far away as possible from the area of the crimes. Meanwhile, there's a young girl who just lost her brand new car, cursing herself for leaving the vehicle with the keys in the ignition. The local Police have been notified but they're at the

Judge's mansion, trying to make sense out of a gruesome and bizarre situation.

Parker pulls off the road and into a small gas station that is closed but has two outside phone booths. The first one he tries to use is missing the telephone. The second works though and he dials Steph's number. She answers after five rings and he is thrilled to hear her voice again.

"Stephanie, it's me, Parker… I need to see you bad."

"Where are you," asks his former girlfriend.

"That doesn't matter, just meet me."

"I can tonight, but I would rather tomorrow around noon. Where did you want to meet up Parker?"

"How about the Woodhaven train station it's near your house. I'll be there at 12 o'clock midnight. I can't wait to see you and hold you… I miss you so much Steph, you don't know what I've gone through; the torment has been unreal. Will you meet me?" he asks.

"I've got to go, I hear my parents coming upstairs. Yes, I'll be there."

"I still love you Stephanie."

"I… love you too," she says crying.

They both hang up. She dries her eyes, and then calls Matlind.

"Recovery, may I help you?" answers the Private Eye. "Hello, Mr. Matlind, it's me, Stephanie."

"Are you alright, you sound a little shook-up," he asks.

"I've been better; Parker just called. He wants me to meet him at the Woodhaven Boulevard Station at midnight and I don't know what to do."

"This might be our only chance. Yes, go there and I'll be somewhere on the platform keeping a low profile and watching his every move. Stay away from the edge and keep your eyes open. I'll give the Police a 'head's up' then call them in when we're ready to close the trap," Matlind says with confidence.

"I don't know if I can' do this John."

"They found the Judge decapitated in his mansion. It's been a clean sweep; the entire Jury is gone now and Parker Wilsone has completed his evil mission. He must be locked up and taken off the street and pay for his crimes against the innocent citizens of society."

"Alright, I'll be on the platform at midnight but I feel like I'm betraying him," she says.

"Maybe you are Steph, but it's certainly for the good of all concerned. Remember, we have reason to believe that he's murdered twelve people in a bizarre Astrological pattern. Parker's got to be taken down."

"Thanks Mr. Matlind, I'll see you then," Stephanie says just before hanging up the phone.

The Private Investigator locks his office door, and then sits back down at his desk. He opens a draw and takes some fresh rounds out, fully loading his handgun. He checks his map after making a series of phone calls. Julie is out sick today so he takes care of some loose ends and office business. That done, he calls Samantha, letting her know of the plan to capture Parker that night. He gives her specific instructions to follow in the event of various outcomes. They are in love and she fears for his life, but she knows that John is an expert at what he does and that this is the opportunity that Matlind has waited for, for a long time. He thinks about the night of the Execution and how circumstances have changed so radically for those involved in the sentencing; innocents who were chosen at random to fulfill their civic duty. He removes his necktie and sport coat, choosing a lighter zip-up jacket; checks his handgun, then replaces the weapon in his shoulder holster. Picking up his keys, the PI turns out the light and locks his office door behind him.

Five minutes after midnight finds Stephanie waiting on the station platform for the train that Parker is supposed to be on. Matlind stands about twenty feet away, partially hidden by a heavily painted vertical steel girder with large square bolts. The Private Investigator is difficult to detect, but can keep Stephanie in his sight.

Parker Wilsone sits in a graffiti-ridden subway car across from a sleeping wino. The train takes a curve and a cheap bottle of Muscatel falls from the bum's overcoat pocket. It slides over to Parker's foot as the train lurches onward. Wilsone picks it up and takes a couple of swigs from the flat-shaped bottle. He makes a sour face as the alcohol taste hits home. The fugitive stands up and checks the wall map while leaning against the door, holding on to the stainless steel pole. Even though he is tenser inside than ever, his body language is definitely laid-back. The train from the city comes around the bend heading into the Woodhaven Blvd. Station. John Matlind opens up the wide newspaper and refolds it, creasing the pages sharply. He glances over at Stephanie who is nervously pacing back and forth near the yellow stripe at the edge of the platform. The train has slowed down and is entering the station. Only a handful of people are on the platform at this late hour when the train comes to a dead stop and the doors open wide. About half a dozen commuters leave the train. Stephanie and Matlind watch but they do not recognize Parker. The March winds are cold though and two of the commuters are wearing hoods. One of them walks slowly down the platform toward Stephanie as Matlind lowers the paper slightly. The man has a goatee and is about Parker's height but it is impossible to tell if it is him underneath the hood. He walks past Stephanie, stopping about ten feet away. Turning around he walks over to her and asks for the time. She looks at her watch and tells the stranger that it's 12:23 (A.M.); that's when he asks, "Did you come alone Steph?"

"Parker, my God, it's you," she says, caught off guard.

"That's right Stephanie, it's me. Here comes the next train, let's take it."

"Where are we going?"

"I have a car parked at Suphin Blvd., we'll drive out to Suffolk."

He notices her repeatedly looking in a certain direction. Turning his head and scanning the platform he recognizes the Detective without even seeing his face. Matlind freezes and the train pulls into the station. The doors open but no one enters as passengers disembark. Matlind waits, then Parker suddenly pushes Stephanie into one of the cars. The doors close and Matlind curses his bad timing. The train still doesn't move. One of the Conductors sees John at the doors of a car and reopens them for him. Matlind quickly gets on board; the doors close and the train rolls out of the Woodhaven Station. He begins to move through the long line of cars as Parker tries to run with Stephanie but let's her go as she is trying to hold him back. When Matlind runs into her car he tells Stephanie to stay there while he tracks Parker down. She agrees reluctantly and he takes off again, following behind Parker about two car lengths. The Detective is slowed down as he gets stuck momentarily between two cars. The fugitive continues running through the dozen railroad cars, one of which holds five gang members going back to their turf. Parker knows that Matlind means business but he still feels that he can elude him and escape. The Private Detective runs into the train car that the gang members are riding in; one of them trips him up as he hurriedly walks past them in pursuit of Wilsone. Matlind falls to the floor, and then recovers as the young 'sharks' move in. He knows just what it's going to be—he's been there before, quite a few times. He deals out a couple of low kicks to his enemies, followed by some high punches and back-fists to their heads. Bang! He gets hit from behind with an open hand on his ear. It hurts like hell but he turns and strikes out with multiple fist attacks, morphing from the hunted to the hunter as he continues to deal out blows to his adversaries. With three down, two run one way as Matlind runs in the opposite direction. This little workout cost him valuable time and energy but he's glad that his old military, empty hand training kicked in. If you were taught well and applied yourself, it would always come back to you… kind of like riding a unicycle. He staggers over to the door and looks out through the glass as the train pulls into the station. After coming to a complete stop, the doors part and Matlind looks out onto the platform. A few passengers step off the train but Parker is not among them. Just then Stephanie enters the car walking with a slight limp. The Detective sees Wilsone step off the train.

"Got to go Steph or I'll lose him."

"Go ahead Matlind, don't wait for me, but be careful… try to take him alive," she pleads.

"Yeah, right," he quips under pressure. "I hope he's tired, because I've got nothing left."

"Go! He's getting away," she yells.

Matlind bails just as the doors begin to close; he runs to the platform railing and sees Parker heading toward the train yard on foot; descending the endless steps he gives chase.

Parker runs down the tracks exhausted, falling a couple of times as he tries to make his getaway. As the fugitive stumbles into the maintenance yard, nearly touching the third rail, he looks behind and sees Matlind closing in on him fast. Wilsone angles off and heads into a deep tunnel. The Detective picks up his trail and cautiously enters the tunnel. Neither one has a flashlight but Matlind waits for his eyes to become accustomed to the darkness. He can faintly hear footsteps moving away from him toward the other side of the tunnel. He begins to follow the sound as the rail yard rats scurry past him in the dark. Eventually, the sound stops and all is quiet. Matlind freezes in the blackness, waiting for the next move. Suddenly, an old piece of frayed rope is wrapped around the Private Detective's neck. The assailant in the murky dark tightens the rope with a powerful grip as Matlind coughs and gasps for air. He rolls his head around and drops down, coming up underneath the adversary. The back of his skull drives up striking the creature in the nose, sending him to the ground and sounds of squealing rats running. Matlind pulls the grisly piece of rope from around his bleeding neck. He steps in the general direction of his fallen opponent, hears a noise and throws a front kick into the dark. His foot strikes Parker's chest, knocking him back on the tracks. The walls grow lighter as a huge three car train enters the tunnel, coming right at Parker who's spread eagle across the tracks. Matlind runs to him without hesitation, and dives, grabbing him and rolling out then pulling Parker over him and onto the pebble strewn ground just as the big train passes within an arms length of the battling rivals, of good and evil.

Stephanie makes a call to the Police from the street below the station; they send out a car to the train yard immediately. She waits for them at the entrance to the maintenance yard for about five minutes and then decides to go in on her own.

Matlind chases Parker out of the tunnel and into the partially lit yard. The killer runs past graffiti-ridden train cars, some of which look like commercial artwork and others that are merely amateur garbage. They are in this yard for cleaning and repainting. As the youth stops to catch his breath he notices one car with a detailed picture of the Grim Reaper complete with a skull face and a large sickle blade in one hand and holding a black cat, in a Halloween stretch, with electrified hair in the other. A giant number 13 has been sprayed on, but there isn't any signature; no one has tagged the Neo Gothic scenario.

"This is it Parker… end of the line," says Matlind as he catches up to Wilsone. "You're sick dude, you were brilliant once, but you went insane. Take a look around Wilsone, can't you see the writing on the wall? This is it, the game is over, it's time to resign." Parker replies with, "Not yet Matlind, I've still got a couple of moves." The Detective draws his pistol and fires one round into the dirt. Parker slowly reaches into his pocket but seems to be missing something as he comes up empty handed.

"Don't shoot him Matlind, it's not worth it," says Stephanie as she walks up behind the Private Eye. The Skull train slowly pulls out between Parker and Stephanie. He can be heard calling her name over the hum of the powerful engines. Parker begins to run slightly ahead of the train as the Police cars drive into the yard. Looking into the window, the fugitive sees the face of Judge Morton as he drives the ghost train. All the dead members of the jury are peering out from the passenger car and looking at the terrified Parker. Each juror has an Astrological symbol displayed on their forehead; they seem to smile through the hazy windows of the train. Parker tries to outrun the ghost train in sheer panic but trips and falls on the rocky ground in the train yard. He rolls, avoiding the train but inadvertently grabs the exposed third rail which sends a fatal surge of electricity through his tortured body. The face of the Grim Reaper passes on as the Judge and Jury have their final look at Parker James Wilsone, as he gazes out of dying eyes to see Simon Watson, the murdered black man, wearing a railroad engineer's uniform and slowly swinging a lantern from side to side, as the ghost train makes it's way down the long line of winding tracks. The lantern light grows dimmer as night becomes dawn in the railroad yard. Sounds of the ambulance's sirens are becoming increasingly louder as this insane drama draws to a close. The cops search the area, finding a loaded derringer that was taken from Judge Morton's house along with a final note for Stephanie, the contents of which shall remain private at this time. As Matlind watches how this whole thing plays out, he recalls the meeting at Dr. Chang's and how all the pieces seem to fit now. The reign of terror is over.

Parker was laid out in a funeral home in the city. Matlind was one of the few people there when Stephanie went up to his coffin and cut off his ponytail with a scissor. The Private Detective was shocked but in a way understood. Parker was denied burial in a Catholic cemetery even though he never lived to be convicted of the thirteen murders.

Four years later, Matlind's Recovery business is doing great. He hired young Kevin Lincoln after he received his two year B.A. Degree from Nassau College. John and Samantha married after the Horror Scope case was officially closed when it came to light that Parker's tier mates and Chess students, Jake and Spider, who were in for other crimes, stuck the knife in old Simon Watson that night in the city alleyway; Lee Roy Spyder actually did the deed; a fact that just serves to underline this whole strange chain of events. Detective Lawrence cracked the case.

Samantha's parents gave her and John the house on Meadowrue Lane when they retired to Rio Rancho in Albuquerque, New Mexico. John had a big addition put on the structure, adding bedrooms, a den and bathrooms. The Matlind's are happy residing in Exurbia. They attend their local Church, St. Bart's, every week, but also never miss the Eve of All Hallowed Saint's Ball. They have a beautiful three year old daughter named Cyndi born June 2nd, and Samantha's twin sister's room is still the same as she left it, except for the fresh flowers. Cyndi likes to go there and play with her twin dolls sometimes. As for Stephanie, she's living in Florida now, with her young son James Parker.

The city and suburbs are back to normal, if you want to call it that, and life continues on beyond the scope of horror that an Astrologer of great genius who joined forces with the Devil unleashed on those who wrongly accused and convicted him of a brutal crime that he did not commit. True, Parker escaped execution, but it was only a reprieve because there is no pardon from the inevitable finale.

→»≪←

Time passes quickly as the Matlind Family grows. John and Samantha have been married for seven years now. They have two children. Their daughter Cyndi is six years old and son Jack is age three. Matlind's private eye recovery business has grown with the detective's reputation for coming through in the clinch. The 'Horror Scope' case was closed almost a decade ago, but the memories of Sam's sister's death still linger in the house on Meadowrue Lane.

It's Saturday morning at the Matlind home. The kids rouse their sleepy parents, all but pulling the top sheets from the bed. Breakfast is on the table forty-five minutes later and the cartoon shows have commandeered the large television screen in the family room. Cereal, pancakes and mom's delicious cinnamon toast grace the round table in the dining area. John's at home today, taking care of some put-off repairs around the house. He works on various projects until mid-afternoon when the children take their naps. He and Samantha sit outside on the large wooden deck, drinking mint flavored iced tea as they enjoy the beautiful day.

"You know what next week is, right?" asks Samantha.

"Do you mean the anniversary of Woodstock?" he says, having some fun with her. "No... hello... it's our ninth wedding anniversary John."

"I knew that," he assures his bride. "Have you planned ahead and set up something special for it?"

"What did you have in mind Sam?"

"I want you to come up with something unique and special."

"OK... how about two tickets to paradise dear?"

"We went to Atlantis on our honeymoon," the attractive brunette states. "Which paradise are we talking about here?" she says as she moves her chair closer to her husband.

"How about the Big Island? How does that hit you?" John inquires. "You mean Australia… it's so far away though."

"No, I mean the 'Big Island,'" he repeats, raising his hand with the thumb and small finger extended.

"HAWAII!" she shouts out in surprise. To which John nods his head, smiling.

"I love you so much," she says as she hugs him excitedly.

"I love you too, babe," says John before kissing her sweet lips. "What about the kids, it's a long trip?"

"This is our second honeymoon."

I've arranged to fly into Albuquerque. Cyndi and Jack will stay with your parents in Rio Rancho while we go on our Hawaiian adventure. We fly into L.A. for a two-hour layover, then it's another five-and-a-half-hour leg to Hawaii. It's all set, start packing sweetheart." John produces the airline tickets from his back pocket, placing them on the table. Samantha quickly picks them up saying, "Be careful, you'll get them wet. I'll put them in my lingerie drawer for safe keeping."

"They'll certainly be happy in there, Sam." She stands up and sits on his lap, planting a hot kiss on his still smiling face. The sound of their son Jack waking up shatters the bubble.

"We'll continue this discussion later," she says as she stands to go into the house.

"Definitely," he replies as Samantha turns and says, "Thanks," blowing him a kiss, which he pretends to catch on his cheek.

Kevin Lincoln picks up the phone answering, "Recovery," from Matlind's office. There is no voice on the other end of the line and the caller ID number doesn't come up. He waits but doesn't hear anything, then hangs up. This is the third call of this nature this week, he wonders if this is a pattern. Kevin will be running the office when his boss, John, goes on vacation. He's been learning the business from the bottom up and he wants to make it his career. He loves the investigative work; he always did. It's Julie's day off and Lincoln is taking care of the usual business. One case in particular really interests him. It deals with a long Japanese sword that was sold a number of times. The value of the heirloom increased as it changed hands and more information surfaced about the cherished blade, supposedly once owned by an Emperor in the land of the rising sun. The prized sword rose in value to $50,000 and was purchased through a private dealer on the West Coast. Shortly after the change of ownership, the cherished Samurai sword was stolen. That was over a year ago and the costly antique hasn't resurfaced since. Lincoln pulls up some general history on these weapons, trying to educate himself in this field that is new to him. Working on a full-time basis with Matlind showing him the ropes has allowed Kevin to really focus on a special kind of job for the first time in his young life. The phone rings and it's Matlind checking in with Kevin, who tells him about the sword and the mysterious phone calls. John's thinking is preoccupied with visions of Hawaii now and he's finding it hard to focus on anything else at this time; he'll deal with it when he gets back in three weeks.

The next morning Kevin drives the Matlinds to the MacArthur Airport Southwest terminal. They all say a quick goodbye and he wishes them a safe trip and great vacation. John and Sam and the kids enter the small airport to begin a two hour wait for the departure of their flight to New Mexico. Their plane touches down that afternoon on the Southwest runway. After renting a mid-sized car they drive up to Starlit Road in the development known as Rio Rancho, where Samantha's parents have lived for the last decade. Samantha's dad is standing there, waiting to greet them and help unpack the luggage.

Sam hugs her mom, who she hasn't seen for two years. The kids are already running through the house, taking over the grandparents who are easily wrapped around their little fingers. After a while the family settles down for a small meal, catching up on all that's happened since they last saw each other. The next morning Samantha and John sneak away for breakfast burritos at the famous Frontier eatery on Central across from the University of New Mexico. After a great meal and viewing of many southwestern paintings, they cross the wide street to check out the school's extensive gift and book shop. On the way back to the car some grungy guy asks Matlind for some spare change. The detective snaps out a crisp dollar bill to the thankful panhandler.

The following morning granddad drives John and Sam to the airport for the flight to L.A., saying their goodbyes, the two walk into the terminal like kids on an adventure trip.

After checking in at the ticket counter, John and Sam have a drink and a bite to eat at the airport grill. They talk about their options once they reach the Big Island. They walk through the airport after the meal, checking out the small shops and large magazine store. John and Sam share a coffee as they wait to board the flight to

Hawaii, he buys a book titled "Never Scratch a Tiger with a Short Stick."

Their backs are pinned to the seat as the big jet guns its engines down the runway. In a short while they leave the California coast heading out to the mid-Pacific Ocean where the Big Island awaits them for their second honeymoon.

They are happy and kick back with a few drinks. Samantha watches the in-flight movie while John naps with the headset on. The aircraft cruises at 35,000 feet with nothing but clouds and water below them; this will prove to be a trip that the young couple won't soon forget.

Six hours later they arrive at Kona Airport. Driving away form the auto rental in a PT Cruiser they head to the King's hotel in the Kona District, where they will spend the first four days of the vacation. The weather is perfect here on the sunny side of the island. They spend the day in the pool, then shopping and having lunch. Returning to the ocean view hotel room they prepare for the big Luau, one of the best on the island.

They arrive early for the VIP seating and a photograph before entering the outdoor dining area. Choosing seats close to the small stage they chat with another couple at their table. John goes to the open bar but can only get two drinks at a time. After three quick trips they are set up for a while. Another couple joins them. They are locals who live up north in Kamuela and attend this Luau at least once a year. Dr. Sam is into Oriental medicine and his beautiful wife Lily is a teacher of Japanese floral art (Ikabana). The others at the table are Maria and Larry, on vacation from San Diego. He's a pilot and she works in the hospital administration office. Everyone is on their second drink as the moon rises over Kana town and a re-enactment of the arrival of King Kamehameha in a small boat begins the cultural festivities of the evening. Necklaces of tiny shells are passed out to all of the guests as how to chop open a coconut is demonstrated by the performer who will later do the traditional fire dance. Another round of drinks is brought to the table as the guests fill their plates with the incredibly delicious varieties of food on the steam tables. Fish and fruit abound along with other island delicacies; huge bowls filled with yellowtail *poke* are displayed next to the mysterious tasting *poi*. Interesting conversation fills the night air at John and Samantha's table as Dr. Sam says to John's pretty wife, "You and I have the same name." She smiles, showing what a perfect set of teeth looks like. "I know," she answers. "What are the odds of that?"

"What type of work do you do Mr. Matlind?" Lily asks. "Please call me John, Lily. I do recovery work as a private investigator. I used to be on the job in Suffolk County, that's Long Island, but I got injured one night on a foot pursuit and had to retire early. I keep busy though; we have a lot of interesting cases come in from time to time."

"What do you recover primarily John?" asks Dr. Sam.

"Pretty much anything, including people," the PI replies.

"How long are you here for John?"

"Our vacation is another week, but that's not carved in stone."

"Are we extending our trip dear?" asks Samantha.

"I may have need of your services if time is not an issue" says Dr. Sam. "Do you need something recovered doctor?"

"I do but it might be difficult."

"That's nothing new. What are we talking about?" asks Matlind.

"We're talking about an heirloom; an unusual Japanese sword, that is also said to be cursed."

"Interesting... go on Sam," encourages Matlind.

"Back in your home state of New York a rare Samurai sword was sold for $200 in 1970 in a small antique shop on 2nd Avenue in Manhattan. The owner was at a lunch meeting with an important client when his nephew, Edward Greene misread the tag with a faded $2,000 price on it. When the owner of the store came back from lunch, he was shocked to find out what had transpired. There was no record of the purchaser's name or address as it was a quick cash transaction. Edward also mentioned that he remembered the buyer of the sword having been in the store before. He offered a general description of the man but there were no defining characteristics."

"Why was the weapon unusual?" asks Matlind.

"Because of its extra-long length and the fact that it was believed to be the death sword of a 'Ronin' who was a 'blade for hire' during the seventeenth century. He is said to have been killed in his sleep by his own sword at the hands of a cowardly criminal he was seeking to collect the bounty on."

"Great story, Sam, but where is the sword now?"

"We believe that it is on the islands in the Hawaii chain.

That is why I mentioned the time element."

"You've definitely got my interest, Sam."

"Why don't you come up to our house in Kamuela tomorrow and we can talk more about the case" says Dr. Sam as the fire dancer enters the small stage to the sound of the building drum beats. Pele, the goddess of fire weaves her spell into the night of festivities.

The next day the Matlinds drive up the Big Island's west coast in their rented PT Cruiser.

"I like this car, it's different," John says to Samantha.

"It's got a great nostalgic body," adds Sam. He looks over at her and smiles as his eyes sweep down to her tan legs. ''And you look good behind the wheel, you'd make a great Cell Cop John."

"No way Sam, there's not enough action for me; that's not my cup of tea."

"What about your friend Frank?"

"Madson? Well he started by driving the Mayor around but after the cell cops formed, he ended up as a Sky Marshall and foiled a major follow up plane jacking... that's where the action was for him."

"Is he still active in that field?" asks Samantha.

"I haven't seen him in years, he might be retired or is back to writing cell phone tickets."

They continue to drive up through Parker Ranch where they pass beneath a giant rainbow that seems to divide the Big Island in half, with the East Coast being the wet side down through the Hilo area and the opposite, or Kona Coast, the dry sunny side. Making a quick stop they buy Maui style potato chips and the local brand of bottled water. Back in the Cruiser they turn left and head up into the heights to Dr. Sam and Lily's house where the dew-like mists permeate the landscape. They park in the driveway behind a classic red and black T-Bird. Lily comes out to meet the couple, telling them that Dr. Sam is finishing up his daily practice of Wu Tai Chi in the Oriental Garden which is surrounded by lush vegetation. They enter the high beamed ceiling house and relax with some kind of fruit drink with a taste that they've never experienced before. Dr. Sam walks in from the *lanai* and bids them good morning. They sit down to a light breakfast that Lily has prepared and talk about the island.

"So, what do you folks think of our island of adventure so far?" Lily asks.

"It's an incredible place," John replies.

"People save for years just to come here for ten days of their lives—and it's your backyard," Samantha says.

They walk out on the high back deck after breakfast and look out on the green rolling hills.

"I had a great uncle in Scotland, where we stayed for two summers when I was in my teens," says Matlind, "and this scenario brings back a lot of forgotten old memories." They look out on the rain shadow in silence for a while, watching the drizzling mist as the fine water vapor moves across the rolling green hills and meadows. They watch from the high porch as several cows and horses meander by the windblown pines.

"You know, John, this island is like a big circle, like the yin/ yang symbol with Kona on the West Coast or sun side at about eight o'clock and Hilo on the right, windward side where the rain is frequent, at about three o'clock. A giant rainbow crosses the island at the north point of twelve o'clock. It's all laid out so systematically by the Creator."

"It certainly is Dr. Sam," says Matlind. They walk back into the house and Dr. Sam brings the PI into his office where they take seats amongst the many Polynesian artifacts. Dr. Sam begins to tell John a story about the unusual Japanese sword.

The front door opens and Lily and Sam's daughter comes in with her boyfriend, who is carrying packages for her. They meet Samantha and then go upstairs to the girl's room.

Dr. Sam and Matlind talk about the sword in the den.

"As I told you John, the Samurai sword in question was mistakenly purchased for $200 (it was faintly marked at $2000) but the buyer knew what he had, or at least thought that he did. He managed to re-sell the blade at $5000 to a shrewd collector. The new owner did further research then sold the weapon to an elderly Japanese man in California for $25,000. This man, Norobu, was an old friend of my wife's brother and contacted me about a buyer in Maui who was interested in purchasing the blade for $50,000. The deal was agreed upon and the rare sword was shipped..."

"What made the weapon so rare, Sam?" asks Matlind, cutting in. "The weapon was unusually long. It is called an *Odachi* ... very valuable."

"Excuse me," says Matlind, "go on."

"The transaction was completed. The sword was bought by an Hawaiian surgeon for $50,000 and we were told by certain collectors that the blade could probably sell again for up to $100,000.

"Where's the ceiling on something like this?" asks the detective. Dr. Sam looks at him eye to eye and says, "Where's the ceiling on the sky?

"Enough said on price," echoes Matlind.

"Then one night while the doctor was attending a big luau with his wife and brother, a thief broke into his house and stole the long sword, along with a valuable *netsuke* and some *tsubas*. Word got out that a man named Ogawa, who had a reputation as a cat-burglar, stole the goods. He was also a ranking black belt in Japanese Karate." Dr. Sam removes a photograph from the top drawer of his desk and passes it to Matlind. It is a picture of a Karate man doing a flying side kick at the beach with the waves in the distance below him.

"So, this is our man?" asks Matlind.

"Yes, that's him John. Come meet my daughter and her boyfriend." They walk out of the den into the big living room. Sam's daughter enters the room and her beauty takes the detective's breath away. Her name is Lauraloha and her fiancee is Kai Lan, whose grandfather Kim owns a big soy sauce factory on the mainland in California. Kai is an avid surfer who runs a small surf shop in Kona. They make a nice young couple who radiate joy and freedom of living in this magic tropical place.

That night after a steak dinner up in Parker Ranch, John and Samantha drive back down to the King Hotel in Kona town. They bring in dessert from the ABC store and head up to their room. This trip is a second honeymoon for them and they're lovin' every day on the Big Island.

An hour passes and Samantha steps out of the bathroom; her husband turns off the television. She walks halfway over to the bed and drops her silk robe to the carpeted floor.

"Wow, you look outrageous, Sam."

"Thank you dear... and you look pretty good yourself."

"Com 'ere," says John in a soft voice.

She slides into the king-sized bed like a sleek jungle cat on the prowl. They embrace, kissing thoroughly as the two lovers roll across the large mattress. Outside, beyond the balcony, the tropical night winds move the palms back and forth in the currents of nature and light of the honey colored moon graces the incoming waves.

The next morning Samantha and John have a great breakfast in the King Hotel's large dining room. Afterwards, they stroll through the many lobbies and hallways learning about the island's history and culture. The exhibits show archaic tools and watercraft that have been used in Hawaii for years; it's an education and serves to enhance the romance of the entire trip. They hold hands as the couple emerges into the soft sunlight of another beautiful day. John and Samantha walk across the short expanse of beach to the old seawall where an elderly turtle is basking in the sun's rays. They check him out until the senior citizen quietly withdraws into his shell. Climbing the short run of steps, they go up to street level, merging with the new-day influx of tourists in the special town of Kona. There are many cool shops in this area; it's a cakewalk with a fresh brewed local coffee, possibly the best any land has to offer. Matlind flips through the tropical shirt rack as Sam decides on which sarongs she likes the most. As John turns to the window he notices a middle-aged Japanese man browsing from the street who looks familiar … but from where? Matlind thinks of Dr. Sam – and then OGAWA! The man outside the window turns and walks away from the village, crossing the street to the waterside.

Matlind quickly tells Sam and then is out the door and picking up Ogawa's trail. He briefly loses sight of his prey but regains visual contact as the man goes off on an overgrown trail near the beach. Ogawa turns and quickens his pace up a short grade then disappears into a three-foot cave, an old lava hole that runs to the bluff overlooking the water. The detective looks around and finds the opening of the ancient cave. He peers in to see a faint light in the distance but cannot determine if anyone is in the underground hollow because of the slight winding of the time-worn tunnel. Matlind enters the tube (against his better judgment) and begins to walk in a super low crouch which doesn't work after five minutes.

He kneels down and gets fragments of the ceiling underneath his knees as he crawls tediously through the cave on the trail of (who he believes to be) Ogawa. Pausing, he listens for any movement. Matlind hears a faint scraping in the tube about fifteen feet ahead, he also notices that the tunnel is narrowing. Turning a corner, he sees a figure lying on his stomach at the end of the volcano tube. The man is silhouetted by the overcast sun outside. Matlind approaches slowly, then stops. He takes a shot and calls out, "Ogawa?" but there is no response. The Private Eye thinks of an old movie in which Charlie Chan asks a group about a murder. When no one speaks Chan says, "Silent answer sometimes loudest." Matlind begins to close in on Ogawa, knowing that if it wasn't him, he probably would have told his real identity. The mystery man moves closer to the edge of the tunnel as Matlind closes in on him. But the gumshoe knows his opponent and has been given a heads-up on his kicking prowess, especially in a confining situation like this one. Getting in range, Matlind makes a grab for the guys ankle anyway. The foot is withdrawn immediately and then strikes out and downward. John gets his left hand in the way of the thrust kick by the shoeless assailant.

"It's a long way back, Mister, do what you have to do," says the detective. The man pulls himself forward to the edge of the tunnel. He looks down, waiting for a minute or so, then pushes his body forward and out, after uttering the word *Abayo*. Matlind hears a splash and crawls to the edge of the tube. Looking over he sees a drop of about twenty feet to the tide pool of incoming waves … there is no sign of the diver. It is hard to tell if rocks lie beneath the surface of the water below. One would have to know the area and the tides to exit this volcanic tube with confidence. Matlind was unsure. Maybe if he had seen the mystery man in the water he would have taken the plunge and pursued him, but that didn't happen so John Matlind begins the trek back to the opening in reverse; his bare knees are torn up and bleeding from the ceiling debris that crusts the floor of the tube. It's a long haul back and he keeps wondering if indeed it was Ogawa, the man who possesses the valuable *O dachi* sword. Matlind finally reaches the opening and steps out falling to the ground because his legs are not right due to bad circulation. Stretching out in the vegetation he gets the blood flow moving again. He is thinking how good that water would have felt on his knees if he had jumped.

Samantha has the cell phone, but John left his in the room, not foreseeing this tangent on their journey, an interesting digression, if in fact it was Ogawa, the keeper of the special sword. As John makes his way back to the hotel room his bedraggled state causes a few of the tourists to turn their sunbaked heads. When he arrives at the room, he hears the shower running. Five minutes later the water is turned off and Samantha is carefully drying off her shapely body.

'I'm back, Sam," says John.

He hears a muffled, "What happened to you?"

"I'll tell you when you come out. I need to get into the shower soon."

The door opens and Samantha steps out wearing the classic Marilyn Monroe white terrycloth bathrobe. Her face takes on an expression of concern as she sees John's bleeding legs.

"It's a bit of a story that I'll tell you after I get cleaned up, hon."

"Go ahead get in the shower, babe." She walks across the spacious room then turns back to her husband who's removing his soiled clothing. "Feel better," she says as the attractive brunette flashes him. The private eye looks over at her as he steps in the shower, "Sweet!" The torrents of cleansing water rush over Matlind's semi-battered body. The soap burns his shins and knees; his elbows took a beating too. He wondered if the mystery man was Ogawa. If not, why would he run and escape like that.

John and Sam discuss the unusual events of the day over a delicious dinner. She drinks a 'Sea Breeze' while John has a few glasses of his beloved Merlot. They'll be leaving Kona tomorrow and plan to drive up the coast for another visit to Dr. Sam's and Lily's house in the heights before they head east around the top of the Big Island to the volcano region near the town of Hilo.

The following morning begins with a great breakfast in the adequate hotel dining room, then some last-minute shopping in the

Big Island store. Everybody's buying Crocs in the new shoe craze but Sam's not into them. They load up the car and cruise out of Kona and up to Parker Ranch and Kamuela.

Arriving at Sam and Lily's home is a comforting feeling after that incident yesterday. Matlind tells the doctor about the mystery man, who he thinks is Ogawa and how he made his daring escape. He also remembers that the stranger said something before jumping into the water, and thinks it was *Abayo*.

"I got a call from the Aikido teacher who knows Ogawa. He told me that Ogawa wants to destroy this sword and the curse that goes with it. Ogawa is very paranoid now and imagines people stalking him all the time. Did you get a good look at his face John?"

"Yes, I first saw him looking in a shop window while I was inside."

"Did he have a small mole on his cheek bone just below the right eye?"

"It's hard to remember that, Sam."

''Anyway, *Abayo* is the last thing that Toshiro Mifune says in the movie *Sanjuro* to a group of young Samurai who want him to be their teacher. *Abayo* is like a final goodbye."

"Unless we meet again" says Matlind.

''All I know now is that he's trying to get rid of the weapon, by what means I know not. You are welcome to spend the night here and then drive over to Hilo tomorrow afternoon so that you can see the island as you travel."

"I might take you up on that doctor. Hey Sam, the doctor's offered us the guest room for the night."

"That would be great, is it OK with you, Lily?"

"We'd love to have you stay."

"In that case I'll grab some luggage from the car," says Matlind. "Get my small bag John, please."

"Sure hon." The wind was up that night so Dr. Sam lit a nice fire in the stove to take the chill off. They sat around telling stories and drinking wine. Dr. Sam had recently found a pricey aerator in a little wine shop in Havi. They poured the liquid through it and into their glasses and it actually made the merlot taste better, cleaner… hard to describe. Kai and Lauraloha show up at about ten and retreat to the basement apartment where they are currently staying. The giant tank is kept down there that houses the large exotic Arowana fish who has been Kai's pet for a long time. Kai loves the ocean and all the things pertaining to it as much as he loves Lauraloha. Upstairs, Dr. Sam and John discuss Ogawa and the cursed sword.

"That might have very well been him today. You'll probably never see him again, let alone the sword." Sam throws another log in the fire chamber of the stove, "That's it for me, see you in the morning, John."

"Goodnight Doctor." Lily is almost asleep in her bedroom while Samantha watches the local TV channels in the guest room, learning about the history of Pele and the forming of the chain of islands that is Hawaii. Kai comes upstairs to the kitchen to forage around for a snack. "How's it going? says Matlind from across the room."

"Everything's good… and you?"

"Couldn't be better, what a great place you live in, Kai."

"Yeah, I consider myself very blessed."

''Are you looking for something to drink? You must drink a lot of fruit juice here, huh?" asks John.

"No, actually I only drink water or Heineken," replies Kai. "I've got some decent Merlot over here."

'Tm not into wine but I'll have a small one with you." Two glasses later they're talking about surfing."

"My two buds jetted down to Tahiti to surf this spot where the shore breaks over gnarly shallow coral beds. It's such a steep drop that the waves tube out for long durations—it's sick. If you wipe out, they squeeze lime on your coral wounds and it burns like hell, but you got to do it."

"What's it like when you lock into a pipeline wave like that?"

"I don't want to get metaphysical, bro', but it transcends space and time. You just feel so stoked being in that freedom corridor and riding on the natural energy of those awesome sets. You cruise inside the barrel… and you're there."

"Sounds like a special place," says Matlind. "It's like riding on the roof of a locomotive traveling at top speed. It's a major rush… not for everyone," he laughs to himself. Matlind begins to understand the respect that the natives have for nature and its powerful elements on these sacred islands.

"How long does it take to really be a strong surfer?" asks John while pouring himself another glass of the vineyard juice.

"There's all kinds of surfers. You've got the average hot-dogger, who can rip it up when he wants to and then you got the high wall crew who do the toe-ins on jet skis when the storm swells bring in the wave called 'Jaws' to Maui. They find themselves riding down a vertical seventy-foot wall, then if they make it to the base of the wave, they can transit through the giant tube of ocean water barreling in from the Northern Sea. It's an awesome groove to be in—it's like the nautical womb. When you exit, you're born again and return back to the shore. Bottom line is that you have to make it become a genuine part of your lifestyle. To me, you're not a surfer until you've rode ten thousand waves."

Matlind quietly ponders what Kai has just said. They look into the fire in silence. The next day John and Samantha say their goodbyes and drive off towards Hilo and Volcanoes National Park. When they arrive in the area the couple visit some of the sites in the Park, deciding to view the lava after sundown. They have a light late lunch before they begin the drive down the Chain of Craters Road, which ends at the ocean where the road was closed by lava flow years ago.

After parking the car, they use the restrooms and begin to walk across the petrified black rocks, which were once hot lava, now frozen in time. Stopping to take photographs at the famous Sea Ardi, they embrace, kissing soulfully as the Pacific Ocean wind whips their hair in all directions. Moving on along the coast they head for the continuing lava flow in the East Rift Zone where the steam hisses from the rocks like Pelé's breath. The black rocky surface is ever-changing, and the footing can be tricky as there are no existing paths. This is also not the place for sandals or flip-flops as many crevices exist. Flashlights, bottled water, snacks and band aids need to be carried also. Almost everyone has a cell phone now and that could be the difference between life and death out here in 'no man's land.'

The sun is beginning to set and the many scattered travelers can be seen in silhouette as their flashlights are brought out to guide their careful steps in this strange new environment. The rocks seem to go on forever, but the scattered visitors are hopeful that the bright red lava will be flowing this night. Twenty yards ahead a clump of people navigate the increasingly channeled lava plates as the darkness blankets the landscape. One of them carries what looks like it might be a fishing pole inside of a navy-blue cloth case, it appears to be about six feet long in silhouette. What else could it be? Perhaps a scientific instrument for measuring the depth of the crevices in past lava flows. As they get closer to the site, the volcanic fumes that the Rangers warned them about become evident in the night air. John and Sam slow down a bit as the group that was in front of them pauses to take a brief rest before going to view the lava flow, which is running well this evening. There is an unwritten law regarding the taking of pieces of rock from the barren landscape. Many who have brought home small volcanic rocks found it necessary to mail them back to the park complaining of unusual bad luck. These tourists feared that the stones held a curse against those who would remove them from the sacred grounds of the Big Island. Matlin notices a man having a cigarette in the shadows. As the man stands up with his long cloth case John catches a quick glimpse of his face. Something about the stranger reminds the detective of the mystery man who took refuge in the lava tube, but why would he be here? As the group starts to move again Matlind tells Sam about the stranger. They close the gap between them as the bright pinkish red volcano flow comes into sight. Matlind calls Dr. Sam on his cell phone and tells him about the man he thinks might be Ogawa.

Dr. Sam responds by cautioning Matlind about the stranger and speculates that, if in fact it is their man, he might be trying to get rid of the cursed sword once and for all. John tries to get closer but the man clutching the cloth case moves away from the group and towards the high sea cliffs overlooking the ocean.

Matlind tells Samantha that he is going to follow the stranger and to wait for him there (thinking to himself "What are the odds of this situation coming to light?"). The stranger drops into a channel in the rocks and descends the craggy mass of stone and mineral deposits down to the water near the hot lava as it dumps out into the sea. The shadowy figure turns to see Matlind behind him and in one quick move he pulls the long sword in a bright red scabbard from the cloth case and heads for the lava flow. Matlind closes fast fearing that Ogawa will destroy the antiquated blade in the hellish heat and lava fire.

Drawing the sword with some difficulty, the Japanese Karate expert slashes out at Matlind who dodges the first cut but then gets sliced across the top of his left arm. The detective picks up a ten-pound rock and heaves the stone at Ogawa. The fat rock catches the man in the lower part of his legs, causing him to fall to the warm petrified ground. Matlind pounces on the Japanese and attempts to take the naked bladed sword from his hands. Ogawa's grip is strong though and they wrestle around trying to gain possession of the lethal Samurai blade. Ogawa rips the weapon from Matlind's hands and throws it near the running lava.

The detective trips him up and runs for the sword. As he grasps the hilt, Ogawa kicks him in the face, opening up a cut above the detective's eye. John turns his back as Ogawa attacks full force; he drops down and sticks the point of the sword out. Ogawa is impaled at the stomach! He staggers back as Matlind yells "NO!" but he can't reach him in time and the Karate man falls slowly backwards into the rushing river of burning molten lava. Ogawa with the cursed sword through his body is immediately decimated by the power of the goddess Pelé and is washed into the incoming waves of the Pacific Ocean. The detective steps back from the intense heat, bidding his adversary goodbye, ''Abayo Ogawa.'' Matlind wraps the navy-blue cloth case around his bleeding arm while using the empty scabbard as a walking stick to get back up to the top of the channel where his wife is upset and waiting for him.

"John, your face is bruised and swollen, what's going on, are you alright?" she asks with urgent concern.

"It's over… this is all that's left." He holds up the bright red lacquered scabbard from the unusually long sword.

"Dr. Sam is on his way."

"We have to notify the local authorities about this bizarre incident," says John Matlind as he walks with his arm draped over Samantha's shoulder and uses the long scabbard as a makeshift crutch. When they return to the car he collapses in the back seat. Samantha follows Dr. Sam to the first aid station and then the ambulance to the hospital. The special Samurai sword had returned to the element of fire, from which it was forged and born once upon a time in old Japan. Ogawa had come to destroy the sword forever… but the estranged weapon destroyed him as well.

On the day John and Samantha are to leave the Big Island, Dr. Sam and family bid goodbye to their newfound friends and house guests at the Kona Airport. Dr. Sam mentions to John the similarity, like in the film Sanjuro where Mifune compared himself to a sword without a scabbard. That cursed Samurai blade was an awesome weapon with a hex upon it that was too much for it to survive any longer on this planet Earth.

As the commercial aircraft circles around after setting its course, Samantha and her husband take their final look at Hawaii—the Big Island—as they begin to travel back across the Pacific Ocean to LAX in California. Matlind looks down on the slow lava flow to the sea. This will surely be the most incredible vacation they will ever take… what a second honeymoon! From L.A. it's on to New Mexico to retrieve the kids from their grandparents and then it's home to Long Island with some incredible stories to tell. Matlind walks into his office on that Wednesday morning where he is greeted by Lincoln who tells him, "Damn John, you look like you've been in a boxing match."

"It was more like kick-boxing, bro."

Lincoln brings the boss up to date with all that's happened in the last four weeks of the extended vacation.

"And the weirdest thing is that I've finally found a Chess partner, boss."

"Who would that be Kevin?" asks Matlind.

"I don't know their real name but the tag they use is 'REK RAP.'

"Interesting… and have you won any games yet?"

"No, but I'm learning a lot from whoever it is," says Lincoln, enthusiastically.

"What does that name mean to you, bro'?"

"I guess it would be recreation/chat," Lincoln justifies. "Do you know that REK RAP is more interesting when spelled backwards?"

"You mean PARKER?" says Kevin Lincoln slowly. "Elementary, Holmes," comments Matlind.

"What?!"

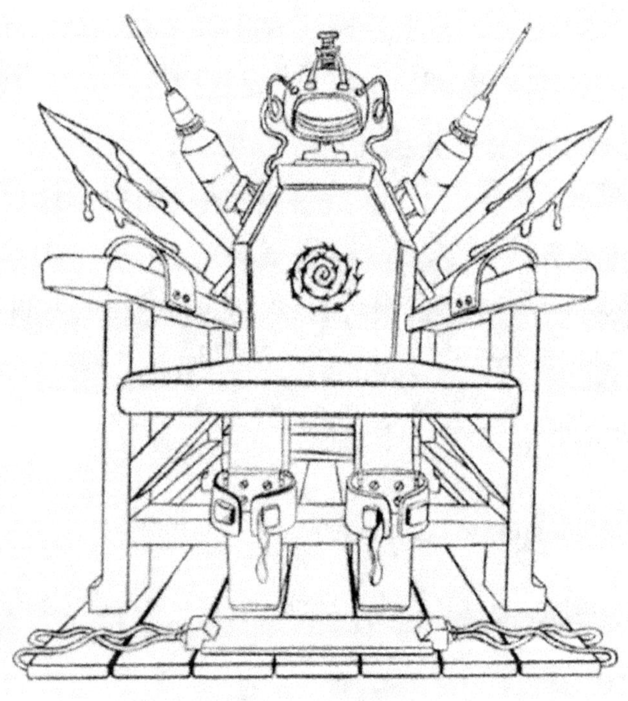

ILLUSTRATION BY TOM SILVINO

Ten Thousand Waves

ILLUSTRATION BY TONY LEONARD